The Rock Star,
the Rooster, & Me,
the Reporter

The Rock Star, the Rooster, & Me, the Reporter

by Phyllis Shalant

illustrations by Charles Robinson

E. P. DUTTON   NEW YORK

for Emily and Jenny,
two characters in their own right

Library of Congress Cataloging-in-Publication Data

Shalant, Phyllis.
   The rock star, the rooster, and me, the reporter / by Phyllis
Shalant; illustrations by Charles Robinson.
      p.   cm.
   Summary: Mandy's adventures in fifth grade include taking
a class trip to her teacher's farm, making a photojournal of
the trip, competing for tickets to a rock concert, and trying to
avoid the class troublemaker, Jonathan.
   ISBN 0-525-44527-7
   [1. Schools—Fiction.]   I. Robinson, Charles, date, ill.
II. Title.
PZ7.S52787Ro   1990   89-33485
[Fic]—dc20   CIP
                                                  AC

Published in the United States by
Dutton Children's Books,
a division of Penguin Books USA Inc.

Published simultaneously in Canada by
Fitzhenry & Whiteside Limited, Toronto

Designer: Martha Rago

Printed in the U.S.A.   First Edition
10 9 8 7 6 5 4 3 2 1

Contents

Mr. Popper

Before I entered the room, I pulled the postcard out of my pocket one last time and checked the number typed there. Sure enough, it matched the one on the door: Room 19. Mr. Popper's room. My hand tingled on the knob. Everyone in school knew that strange things went on in Mr. Popper's classroom. Good strange things.

Lisa Krauss, my best friend, waved at me as I walked in. We hadn't seen each other all summer. She was saving the seat next to her for me.

"You got your ears pierced!" I breathed, as I slid into my chair. "You didn't even write me about it."

"I wanted it to be a surprise. Dad let me do it. My mother was furious when she saw!" she whispered back, excitedly. Lisa's parents had been divorced for three years. She lived with her mom, but every summer she went to stay with her dad. This summer he was living in Maine, about 300 miles from here. His job keeps him moving around a lot.

Mr. Popper sat quietly on top of his desk, waiting for everyone to find a seat. He wore jeans, a flannel shirt, glasses, and had a beard. He looked even older than my dad.

"Welcome to the barnyard," he began. The class laughed. "I'm Mr. Popper, but if you want, you can just call me Mr. P. As some of you already know, I'm a farmer as well as a teacher. During the week, I teach you things you'll need to know in order to grow into capable, independent adults. On the weekends and during the summer, I raise animals and vegetables on my farm. You'd be surprised how much you and the animals and vegetables have in common.

"Next week you'll have a chance to see what I mean. We'll be taking our first trip to my farm."

"Will we get to see you slaughter a chicken?" Jonathan Adler called out. What a creep.

I got stuck with him in my class practically every year. Besides being gross, he is conceited. He thinks he's a genius, but he isn't any smarter than I am.

Mr. Popper ignored him. "This first trip, we'll be picking apples. Then in October, we'll take another trip to begin working on our independent study projects."

"Do you mean like growing our own vegetables?" Stacey asked. I was hoping someone would ask for an explanation.

"Well, that's one of the possibilities. It's called independent study because each person will have to decide for herself or himself what kind of project to work on. Then I'll have a conference with you, and we'll talk about the best ways for you to do your project."

It sounded like fun, but I didn't have much time that morning to think about it. Mr. Popper kept us very busy with math, reading, and all the usual stuff. He even read us the first chapter of *Island of the Blue Dolphins.* He promised to read another chapter each day that we finished our assignments.

In the afternoon, we had a spelling bee. Mr. Popper divided the class into two teams. "Rows one, two, and three stand over by the windows," he said. "Rows four, five, and six, over by the door. Each team should form a single line and count off."

There were cheers from the kids who liked spelling bees (mostly the girls), and groans from the ones who hated them.

"I play this game a little differently than most teachers," Mr. Popper explained. "You will choose the words for each other. Each of you think of a word *you* can spell, but that other people might think is difficult. When it's your turn, ask your opponent the word. If he or she can spell it, that person gets to ask you a word. Naturally, if you miss their word, you're out, and vice versa."

Lisa and I were on the same team, Team A. She was number 11A and I was number 12A. Across the room on the other team, Lacey Lawrence was number 11B and Jonathan was number 12B. Lacey waved at Lisa. The three of us had been in the same class together last year. Jonathan made a creepy pig face at me. *J-e-r-k,* I mouthed at him.

"Maybe you should ask him to spell *oink,*" Lisa whispered.

"Okay, 1A, you begin by asking 1B your word," Mr. Popper started us off.

Stacey was 1A. She'd practically raced up to the front of the line. I didn't know her very well, but you could tell she wasn't shy. "Spell *tonsils,*" she asked Matthew, looking very confident.

"*T-o-n-s-u-l-s,*" Matthew said slowly.

"Wrong," she beamed. "*T-o-n-s-i-l-s.*" Matthew sat down and Stacey went to the back of the A line for round two.

The game went quickly. Kids on both sides were striking out a lot faster than in a regular spelling bee where the words come from a list on your grade level. Lisa gave Lacey the word *Ouija,* which is a kind of board you use to contact spirits. Both Lisa and I can spell it because she owns one. But Lacey spelled it *W-e-e-j-a,* which is how the word sounds, so she was out right away. Then Lisa was out next round on the word *recommend,* which she spelled with two *c*'s. I stayed in each time by spelling *tyrannosaurus, triceratops, stationery* (the paper kind), and *chrysanthemum.* Finally, there was just one person left on each team—Jonathan and me.

It was his turn to ask a word. "Spell *urine,*" he said.

The class started laughing. I looked at Mr. Popper. He was no help. "I don't see what's so funny," he said, calmly. "Go ahead, Mandy, try to spell it."

Jonathan crossed his arms and waited. I thought for a minute. I could spell *urine,* but if I did, I could just imagine all the other disgusting words Mr. P. would probably allow Jonathan to ask me.

I took a deep breath. *"Y-o-u* apostrophe *r-e i-n,"* I spelled.

The class began laughing again. Some kids even applauded. There were also a few shouts of "No fair!"

Jonathan spelled back, smugly. *"Y-o-u* apostrophe *r-e o-u-t."*

"That's not the correct spelling either, Jonathan," Mr. Popper said. "You're both out."

As I returned to my seat, Jonathan's friend Paul leaned across the aisle. "Mandy lost because she can't spell *wee-wee,"* he whispered.

I didn't bother to answer him. I was satisfied with a tie. This time.

When Tammy and I got home that afternoon, we headed straight for the kitchen. Tammy is my little sister. She poured us two tall glasses of Strawberry Snappy, and I took a container of honey-vanilla yogurt out of the freezer. We each plopped half into our drinks, making one of our favorite snacks.

"So how was first grade?" I asked.

"Much better than kindergarten," she answered. "I got a real reader and a workbook. We're even learning vocabulary words. Mrs. Rodriguez calls them our Five-Dollar Words. She's going to give us a new one every week."

"What's this week's word?"

"*Hilarious.* It means very, very, very, very, *very* funny." When Tammy grinned, you could practically see all the way down her throat. Both her front teeth were missing.

We heard Mom's door swing open upstairs. "Are you two home already? I didn't realize what time it was." Mom is a writer and works at home. She writes for a lot of different magazines, but most of her work is for one called *Real Women.* It has articles about what to do if your company won't give you a raise, how to get your kids to cook dinner, and why you need at least two vacations a year. When Dad wants to tease her, he calls the magazine Fake Women.

"How was today, Tam?" Mom asked as she came into the kitchen.

"Mrs. Rodriguez is nice. And I got real homework!" Tammy said, hopping on one foot.

I remembered how I couldn't wait to get homework when I was Tammy's age. I figured by Friday she'd realize how dumb that was.

"How about you, Amanda Panda? Was it a good day?"

"Well, mostly. We're going apple picking at Mr. Popper's farm next week. Then later, we'll go back to begin our independent study projects."

"What's that?" Tammy asked.

"It's a project you think up and then work on by yourself." I sounded as if I'd always known. "You have to get books from the library to help you."

Tammy looked impressed. "What are you going to work on?"

"I don't know yet. We don't have to decide until after the apple-picking trip." But I could see that Tammy was already thinking about what project she would choose, just in case she got Mr. Popper in fifth grade. She's like that.

"What's Mr. Popper like?" Mom asked.

"Well, he's not very strict. He wants us to develop self-control. He says it's an important part of growing up."

"So how did it go?" Mom looked like she wanted to laugh.

"So-so. Naturally I controlled myself. But I had to control that pain, Jonathan Adler, too."

Apple Picking

On apple-picking day, I carried a large shopping bag to school. Mr. Popper was going to let each of us bring home a bagful of apples. When I got to our classroom, he was standing in the corridor talking to Mr. Burke, the music teacher. Inside, it was even noisier than usual. Jonathan and a few of his friends were walking around with their bags over their heads, bumping into people.

"Mandy, over here!" Lisa called. She was standing with Lacey and Sarah Devlin. Lacey and Sarah were best friends. "We're going to try to get seats together on the bus."

"I've got a deck of cards," Lacey said. "We can play slapjack."

"Let's play for candy. I brought M & M's," I volunteered. "Who else has candy?"

Sarah hesitated a moment. "I've got gummy bears. I guess we can use those." She sounded reluctant. "I always lose at cards."

"Don't worry. After we count up our winnings, we'll all share," Lisa said. Lisa can't stand for anyone to be unhappy. "Let's sit up front so maybe Mr. P. will play, too." Sometimes, on afternoons when we'd finished our schoolwork, Mr. Popper would play games like cards or checkers with small groups of kids. He was teaching Jonathan and Paul to play chess. And once on the playground after lunch, he'd surprised us by joining our game of jacks. He was really good!

"Dibs on the first four seats on the bus," Lisa shouted out for the rest of the class to hear.

"Dibs on the last four seats!" Jonathan yelled.

"Everyone take his or her seat," Mr. Popper ordered, as he came into the room. "We have a half hour before it's time to leave. Plenty of time to finish a work sheet."

There was moaning and groaning, but we sat down quickly. No one wanted to be left behind, and we already knew that although it didn't happen very often, Mr. Popper could get pretty angry sometimes. Like when Jonathan and Paul stuffed a smelly sweat sock into Lacey's lunch bag and left it there all morning.

The work sheet was a crossword puzzle about apples. It had clues like "This state produces more apples than any other in the U.S. ———," and "Johnny Appleseed's real name was John ———."

I knew most of the answers because Mr. Popper had already taught us a lot about apples. More than most people would ever want to know. In case you're ever asked, the state is Washington and Johnny Appleseed was really a pioneer apple planter named John Chapman.

Finally a yellow bus pulled up outside. I could see it from my seat near the window.

"Let's go," Mr. Popper said simply. With every other teacher, we'd always had to line up and shut up. But Mr. Popper wasn't much of a believer in lines or quiet. We were supposed to be developing self-control. It didn't always work, but he kept trying.

Since we'd already divided the bus up into

territories, there wasn't much pushing as we boarded. "Remember *Charlotte's Web*?" Lacey asked, as we settled into our seats. Our whole fourth grade had read it last year. "I hope there's a pig like Wilbur." She began dealing out the cards.

"He was so cute." Lisa inspected her hand as she spoke. "But stories always make everything seem better than real life. I don't think Mr. Popper's pigs will be much like Wilbur, or his farm much like the ones in picture books, either." She sounded kind of gloomy. I wondered if her parents had had an argument over the weekend. Even though they'd been divorced for three years, Lisa said they still fought over money. And her.

But Lisa was wrong! Mr. Popper's farm looked a lot like the pictures in the *Little Red Hen* book I had when I was younger. I saw a dusty red barn, a white farmhouse surrounded by bright flowers, a crooked little henhouse, and some animal pens. There were fields planted in rows straighter than I can part my hair, and some just with tall grass growing.

As we got off the bus, we were met by a smiling couple, both dressed in jeans.

"Kids, meet my assistants, Kathleen and

Tom. They live here all year round," Mr. Popper explained.

Kathleen and Tom were tall and suntanned, and looked strong. Kathleen had wavy blonde hair pulled back in a clip and the clearest blue eyes. When she smiled, you could see her perfect white teeth. Tom had his hands in his pockets and smiled at the ground. He seemed shy. Suddenly I wanted to live on a farm.

"We'll just take a quick tour to satisfy your curiosity. Then we'll head out to the apple orchards," Mr. Popper said. "Kathleen, Tom, and I will each lead a group."

I grabbed Lisa's hand and pulled her over to stand by Kathleen. Lacey and Sarah came, too. Jonathan and his pals had joined Tom's group. I looked over at Mr. Popper. Stacey, Danielle, and some of the other kids stood beside him. I was glad we hadn't all deserted him.

Kathleen led us to a pen where two enormous hogs slept in the sunshine. "What are their names?" Lacey asked.

"We call the black-and-white one Domino and that yellow one Wilbur."

Lacey looked amazed.

"You're not the only one who read *Charlotte's Web.*" Kathleen laughed.

There were several smaller pigs in an adjoining pen. A calf stood in another, chewing away.

"Who knows what a cow's cud is?" Kathleen asked. She looked mischievous.

No one answered. "A cow's stomach has four compartments," she explained. "After a cow swallows its food into the first two, it comes back up, and the cow chews it again. That's what the cud is."

"You mean vomit?" Lisa asked in a high, squeaky voice.

"Not exactly. It's a natural part of their digestive process." Kathleen flashed her bright smile.

We started off toward the barn. Suddenly a furious, squawking mop of feathers and claws came rushing at us! I shrieked as it nipped at my legs.

"Red! Get away from here!" Kathleen scolded, shooing a gigantic rooster away from us. "This is Red, Mr. Popper's favorite bird. He just wants to show you who's boss."

Red stood just beyond Kathleen's reach and clucked threateningly. Then he hopped up on the fence around Wilbur and Domino's pen and glared at us. He looked as fierce as any dog I had ever seen.

We just had time to stop by the barn and meet the horses before Mr. Popper called us back together. "We have to get started if we're going to pick apples," he said. "You'll get to see more of the farm on the next trip. Now go climb up onto that tractor bed."

Pushing and laughing, we pulled ourselves up on the long platform. Red got excited and began to chase us again.

"Red, you're a big bully!" Mr. Popper exclaimed, waving the rooster back with a rake.

When we were all seated, Mr. P. climbed onto the tractor and started the motor. We chugged away, leaving Red scolding us noisily, clawing the dust.

Mr. Popper's orchard was bursting with plump, fragrant apples. There was so much fruit, the trees were droopy. It looked like all we would have to do was reach up and pluck what we wanted. Actually, I was a little disappointed. I wanted to climb for my apples. I wanted to lean out a little too far and feel like maybe I could fall.

But the first thing Mr. Popper said as we scrambled off the tractor bed was, "I have only one rule: No climbing. The apples you can't reach will be picked later on by Kathleen and Tom. They've got ladders and picking poles."

We followed him to a bushy tree with low, spreading branches. "In this grove, we've got both Delicious and McIntoshes," he explained. He snapped off a fat apple and held it up for us. "You can see that the McIntoshes are quite round with smooth skin. Now over here are the Delicious."

We trailed him to another tree. It looked the same to me, but Mr. P. picked a second apple and said, "Delicious apples have these four points on the bottom and a more oval shape. Eat all you want while you're picking. That's part of the fun."

Lisa, Lacey, Sarah, and I staked out a McIntosh tree of our own. "Oooh, look how perfect this apple is," Sarah exclaimed, picking a really red, shiny one.

"This one's even better. It's still got a little green leaf attached," Lacey replied, holding up another.

"I've got a great idea!" Lisa said. "Let's have a beauty contest for apples. We can each choose the one apple we think is the best. Then we can line up our favorites and have a competition."

"Who'll be the judge?" I asked.

"Let's ask Mr. P. !"

We ran off and found Mr. Popper. He was

eating an apple and watching Jonathan, Matt, and Paul search for the biggest ones they could find.

"This one's gigantic!" Jonathan said. He had an apple the size of a softball on his out-stretched palm.

"Yeah, it's bigger than the size of Mandy's brain," said Matt, when he saw me.

I ignored him. Lisa told Mr. P. our idea for the contest.

"I'm not entering any stupid beauty contest," Jonathan said quickly.

"How about an ugly contest?" I asked him. "I'm sure you would win."

"Jonathan, you don't have to participate if you don't want to," Mr. Popper said. He turned to Lisa and me. "We'll hold the contest after lunch."

"Let's go tell the others." Lisa tugged my arm.

We were so picky, it took us forever to fill up our bags. I could always find a little something to criticize on an apple: The color was uneven or the apple had a tiny hole; it was too round or too oval; or it had spots. One even had a double bump that looked like my uncle Bernie's nose.

Then I saw it: the perfect apple hanging all

by itself at the end of a branch. Big, red, round, and just out of reach. I tried stretching and I tried jumping, but I couldn't touch it. I knew we weren't supposed to climb, but I really wanted that apple.

Suddenly I had an idea. I took off my wristwatch and put it in a little nook formed by the roots at the base of the tree. Then I stared at the watch for twenty seconds to memorize where it was. That was a trick I had learned in one of my mom's articles.

"What are you staring at?" Lisa asked me. We were the only ones left under the tree. Lacey and Sarah had joined everybody else at two long picnic tables across the field.

"Nothing. I'm through picking," I lied.

"Did you choose an apple to enter?"

"Well, sort of. I'll show you later." This wasn't really a lie, because I *had* chosen one. I just hadn't picked it yet.

As we walked over to the tables, Kathleen drove up in a red truck. She had our lunches and two big jugs of apple cider.

"Okay, time to eat. Find your lunch bags and come on over here," Mr. Popper called out.

Lisa and I grabbed our bags and squeezed

onto the bench next to Lacey and Sarah. I had a peanut butter sandwich, which is all I ever bring for lunch. I wasn't hungry, but I nibbled anyway for a few minutes. Then I announced, "I lost my watch! I think I may know where it dropped off. I'm going to look for it."

"Do you want me to come?" Lisa asked.

"No, don't. I mean, I'll try by myself first. Eat your lunch. If I need you, I'll call."

She shrugged her shoulders and sat back down. I wandered off looking at the ground as though I expected to find my watch. As I left, I heard Lisa explain to Mr. P. where I was going.

The tree was at the far end of the field. I stopped and inspected the ground under two other trees before I got there, just in case someone was watching me. But everyone seemed involved in talking, eating, and comparing apples.

I walked around the back of the tree and began to climb.

The branch my perfect apple hung on really wasn't that high, but the apple was dangling all the way at the end like a Christmas tree ornament. I had to crawl out pretty far to reach it, and the limb was springier than I expected. It groaned and shook as I inched along. I scraped my elbows on the rough bark, and the leaves tickled my nose. A bee buzzed past my ear. I began to think that maybe this wasn't such a great idea after all. I'd climbed the trees in my backyard lots of times, but I'd always stayed close to the trunk. Climbing out on this limb felt much scarier.

I looked over toward the picnic area. Jonathan, Paul, and some of the other kids had already finished their lunch and were playing catch. Mr. Popper was talking to Kathleen.

I inched forward again, and I could almost reach the apple. Just one more foot would do it. But the further out I went, the more the branch trembled. Suddenly, I heard a rustling in the grass below. I looked down and saw a ball roll to a stop beneath me.

Jonathan came running right after it. He bent down, snatched it up, and tossed it back to the others. I held my breath and kept perfectly still. As I lay there, something dropped on my cheek. Carefully, I picked it off and looked at it. It was a fat, hairy caterpillar!

"Ick!" I squealed, and threw it down.

Jonathan looked up. "Hey, Mandy, what are you doing there?"

I clung desperately to the bobbing branch. "What do you think I'm doing? I'm climbing this tree."

"Why?"

"None of your business!"

For a moment, I thought I saw him look at the apple, *my* apple. "What this branch needs is a little shake," he said.

"Get out of here," I hissed, trying to keep my voice low.

But he jumped up high and managed to grab the end of the branch for just a second. There was a dangerous cracking noise, and I let go and fell off, shrieking.

"Hey, are . . . are you okay?" Jonathan asked, staring down at me. "I'll go get Mr. Popper." But he stood there, frozen.

Everyone came running over anyway. I felt stupid lying there like that, but my arms and legs were suddenly so weak, I couldn't get up.

"Are you hurt?" Mr. Popper's face was wrinkled with worry.

"I don't think so," I said, gulping back tears.

"Well, let's just check." While all the kids stood around watching, he had me bend my arms and legs, one at a time. Everything still moved. "Try to sit up. I'll help you." He put an

arm under my back between the shoulders and helped me roll forward.

I sat there for a few seconds. "Okay, now let's get her on her feet," Mr. P. said to Kathleen.

"I can get up myself," I protested.

But Mr. Popper and Kathleen practically carried me to Kathleen's truck. I was so embarrassed, tears rolled down my cheeks.

"That was quite a tumble. How did it happen?" Kathleen asked, as we drove to the farmhouse. Mr. Popper wanted me to rest there until it was time to go home.

"I saw this perfect apple, only I couldn't reach it, so I climbed the tree," I confessed, miserably. "But I wouldn't have fallen if Jonathan hadn't shaken the branch." I left out the part about hiding my watch. My watch! It was still in the orchard! My eyes filled with tears again.

"Don't worry, you'll be all right. It's happened to me, too," Kathleen said. "Kids have been falling out of apple trees for hundreds of years."

I couldn't tell her I was crying because I'd left my watch under the tree on purpose and now I'd lost it for real.

When we pulled up to Mr. P.'s farmhouse, I practically forgot about my watch. I was curious to see what it was like inside. Kathleen swung the door open.

Flowers were everywhere: on the wallpaper, the curtains, the furniture, and the rugs. They were all different colors and patterns, like a crazy, wonderful garden. Kathleen made me stretch out on a sofa covered in big red roses while she brought me some cider and cookies. It made me feel guilty.

Pretty soon, I heard the tractor pull up. The kids all piled into the farmhouse.

"Mandy! Are you okay?" Lisa chirped. She touched a crown of daisies on her head. "I won the apple beauty contest."

"Great," I said, trying to sound enthusiastic.

She grabbed Jonathan's arm and pulled him toward me. "Jonathan found your watch! It was under the tree you fell out of."

"It was right there at the base between the roots," Jonathan said, handing it to me. "You must be blind, besides being such a klutz."

I snatched the watch from his hand. "Gee, thanks," I scowled. I was really glad to get my watch back, but I wished someone else had found it.

"Boy, this sure looks like a good one," Jonathan announced loudly as I put my watch on.

I looked up. He was holding a big, red, round apple. A perfect apple. *My* apple! He smiled at me and took a gigantic bite.

I wanted to clobber him! I wanted to mush him into applesauce! But all I could do was watch him eat my beautiful apple.

When Mr. Popper was finally convinced that I wasn't really hurt, he agreed to let me ride the bus back to school with the rest of the kids. I started to slide into the seat next to Lisa.

"Mandy, I want you to sit here next to me," Mr. Popper called.

I could tell I was in for a lecture.

"You know you weren't supposed to be climbing the trees," he said, once the bus got going. "What made you think you could break the rules?"

"I wanted to pick the best apple," I murmured. "None of the others was good enough to win."

"Do you think winning is that important?"

I knew what he wanted me to say. "I guess not," I answered. But inside I still wasn't sure.

"A much more serious accident might have

occurred. You could have been really hurt—and you could have ruined the day for the whole class," he said. "Would winning the contest have been worth it?"

"I'm sorry," I said. And I meant it. It *was* dumb of me to risk breaking my bones over an apple contest.

"Exercising self-control when you're away from school is as important as exercising it when you're there," he continued. "And respecting the rules is a very important part of self-control. I hope you'll think about that."

"I will," I whispered.

He put his arm around me and gave me a squeeze. "I'm glad you're okay. Next time, stop and think before you act. Now, would you like to play slapjack?"

The Perfect Project

"Now that you've visited the farm, it's time to choose an independent study project," Mr. Popper said on Monday morning. I'd already thought of an idea over the weekend: a chart about the history of farm inventions. I figured whoever invented the picking pole must have fallen out of an apple tree, too.

"There are only two requirements for your projects," Mr. P. continued. "You must consult at least two books about whatever topic you choose, and you must each try to think of something original. Nothing is more boring for a teacher than having to look at twenty projects, all the same. On Friday, I want you to hand in a written description of what you're planning. Then we'll discuss them next week."

The class started to buzz.

Mr. P. held up his hand for quiet. "Using books is only one way to do research. In two weeks, we'll be going back to the farm so that you can collect firsthand information, too. Now you can have five minutes to talk to each other before we go on to our discussion of *The Toothpaste Millionaire.*"

"What are you going to do for your project?" Lisa turned to me excitedly, but she didn't even wait for me to answer. "I'm going to use the foods Mr. P. raises on his farm to prepare a meal for the class!"

"That sounds neat!" I said. "Besides, you're already a terrific cook." Since her parents' divorce, Lisa sometimes made dinner when her mother had to work late. She was great at hot dogs and grilled cheese. Suddenly, my idea for an inventions chart seemed pretty dull. "I'm not sure what I'm going to do yet," I told her.

Lacey came over. "I'm going to try to grow the world's biggest indoor tomato!" she announced.

"Great idea!" I said, as enthusiastically as I could. The inventions chart was definitely out.

"Paul is going to study earthworms," Lacey told us. "He's going to bring in a tank full of them!"

"He's so gross!" Lisa gagged herself with a finger.

"I just decided what I'm going to do. I'm going to study about pigs' intelligence," said Sarah, joining us. "I read they're very smart. Wilbur and Domino can be my two subjects— if I can get them to wake up, that is. Yuki is going to do a diorama about a day in the life of a farmer," she added. "She's going to follow Kathleen around and interview her."

I imagined Yuki helping Kathleen feed chickens, milk cows, and pick vegetables. I wished I'd thought of that idea myself. I wished I'd thought of any of them!

Stacey came bouncing over. Another person with a great idea. It was sickening. "Guess what I'm going to do?" She stood up straight, planted her feet about a foot apart, and stretched her arms out wide.

"You're a scarecrow!" Lisa and I said together.

"You got it! I'm going to make a punk scarecrow for my project! That should scare a lot of crows."

I was starting to feel desperate. Were all the good ideas taken? I had to think up something exciting, too. But what?

"Mom, by Friday I've got to hand in my idea for an independent study project." Tammy and I were at the kitchen table, sampling a recipe Mom was planning to use in an article for *Real Women.* The title was "Don't Run to the Store—Just Open the Cupboard." It was about what to use if you wanted to make a cake but were out of eggs, or what you could put in a taco if you were out of ground beef (anything that saved you a trip, according to Mom).

Instead of Strawberry Snappy, Tammy and I had hunks of cake that Mom had spread with chocolate-mayonnaise frosting. The mayonnaise was supposed to take the place of butter in the frosting.

"Mr. Popper says I should spend this afternoon brainstorming about what I want to do, but I don't know how to begin," I mumbled, the chocolate mayonnaise coating my tongue. You're not supposed to talk with your mouth full, but I couldn't seem to swallow.

"I haven't decided what I'm going to do yet, either," Tammy interrupted. She was mashing her cake with her fork, watching the frosting squish through the tines.

"You're only in first grade!" I burst out. "You might not ever be in Mr. Popper's class."

She pushed out her lower lip in a pout. "I like to be prepared just in case."

"I've got an idea for you," I offered, to appease her. "You could make a chart about the history of farm inventions."

She wrinkled her nose. "Uh-uh. That's humdrum."

"Humdrum?"

Tammy smiled proudly. "It's one of Mrs. Rodriguez's Five-Dollar Words. It means boring."

Mom turned to me. "Go up to your room and nose around. Flip through some books. Daydream. Think about what you like to do best. You'll come up with something."

I pushed my chair back and started for the stairs.

"I guess you didn't like the cake," she observed, looking at my plate.

"Sorry, Mom." The truth was, it was revolting.

"Maybe you'll like the spaghetti with ground carrot and mushroom balls that we're having for dinner."

Harry, our cat, was asleep on my bed. I lay down next to him and stroked his ears. He started to purr. After a while, I got up and walked around my room six times. I looked at my posters of the pigs in high-heeled shoes and long dresses, and of the camel with the glasses and the top hat. I picked up my camera and looked through the lens at my family of stuffed mice.

Mom and Dad had given me the camera for my ninth birthday, when I was still in third grade. Mom said that I was the best photographer in the family. Last summer, the photo store in our shopping mall had held a photography contest, and I'd won an honorable mention. My shot of a goat with a baby bottle in its mouth was displayed in the mall along with the other winners. I'd taken the picture at the nature center, when the goat snatched a bottle from a little kid in a stroller. To go along with the photo, I'd written the caption *"Big Baby Borrows Bottle from Little Buddy."*

Animals, posters, camera—that was it! I had an idea! Maybe I could create a photo journal about the whole class's projects. I could take pictures of the farm, interview the kids while they were working, and show their finished projects. I could read one book about photography and one about reporting.

I ran into Mom's office to try my idea out on her. She had a pencil behind her ear and was staring into space. "Mom, what do you think of me doing a photo journal about the class projects?" I said. "I could take pictures of the farm and the kids working. I'd write a story to go along with it, too."

She nodded while I spoke. "You know, Mandy, when I was about your age I read a book called *So You Want to Be a Reporter?* I can still remember it. Sometimes I think it changed my life. Maybe it's still in the library."

"I'm not really ready to change my life," I said, "but I sure hope they have the book. Do you think you could drive me to the library later?"

"Sure. Give me a few more minutes, and then we can go."

I noticed the recipe for carrot-mushroom balls on top of her desk. "Mom, do you think maybe we can pick up some hamburgers for dinner after we stop at the library?"

Farm Follies

On the morning of the class trip, Dad drove me to school—at 6:15! The day before, Mr. Popper had said we'd have to keep farmers' hours if we wanted to see what farm life was really like. So our homework had been to go to bed early. My dad's no farmer, but he gets up every morning to play basketball with some guys at his gym before work. He says it's the only exercise he gets, because he spends the rest of the day bending over people's mouths. He's an orthodontist.

Lots of kids were already outside waiting for the bus when we pulled up. "I know you couldn't possibly have forgotten anything, Mandy," my father said, rolling his eyes to make me laugh. He gave my hand a little pat as I got out. "Just remember to have fun."

Dad was right. There was no way I could have forgotten anything. I'd awakened at 4 A.M. to make sure I'd packed everything I needed. Film, camera, an extra sweatshirt, baseball cap, pencils and a notebook, lunch, snacks—I was definitely prepared!

Lisa waved to me. She was carrying two giant shopping bags. They were empty except for her lunch and snacks, but she planned to bring them back full of the farm's fruits and vegetables.

Jonathan was just getting out of his mom's car. She handed him something that looked like a shoe box covered in aluminum foil. There was some kind of battery pack on the bottom.

Over the past week, to help plan some pictures for my journal, I'd interviewed a lot of the class about their projects. *So You Want to Be a Reporter?* had a whole chapter on interviewing techniques. I'd even asked Jonathan what he was doing. He gave me his standard answer: "None of your business."

But now that I'd seen his mystery box, I was really curious. Besides, *So You Want to Be a*

Reporter? said if you were turned down for an interview the first time, you should try a different approach. I dragged Lisa with me to the group of boys around Jonathan.

"Is that your project, Jonathan?" I asked, pointing to his foil-covered box.

"Get lost, Mandy!" he replied, in his usual charming way.

Paul and Matthew grinned. About the only thing they like better than watching someone else shoot his mouth off is doing it themselves.

"Suit yourself," I answered, "but I'm writing a photo journal about our trip, and I thought a picture of you and your box would make a great cover shot."

Jonathan went for that one right away. "Oh yeah? Well, I guess my project does deserve to be on the cover of your report," he said. "This is a portable incubator, which I made myself. The light bulb inside the box acts as a source of heat to keep the egg warm until it hatches. The aluminum foil reflects the heat. There's also a thermometer inside the box to help me monitor the temperature. Mr. Popper is going to give me an egg to hatch."

A lot of the kids had gathered around us. I took my camera out and looked through the lens. "Hold the incubator up higher," I directed. Jonathan held it up and said "Cheez Doodles," and I snapped.

The bus arrived and Mr. P. motioned us on. "Hey, Jonathan," I called out, just before I walked up the bus steps. I pointed to my camera. "It's not loaded yet!"

Lisa and I scrambled into a seat and laughed until we nearly died. We could hear the other kids roaring outside the bus, too.

"Look at Jonathan!" Lisa giggled. "Even his ears are on fire!"

I pressed my nose against the window. Jonathan ran over to the bus, jumped up, and slapped his palm against the glass. His mouth was moving, but I couldn't hear what he was saying. It was probably better that way.

Kathleen and Tom were waiting when the bus pulled up. So was Red. They looked happy to see us—Kathleen and Tom, I mean. Red clucked angrily and hopped about, but he didn't attack. Mr. Popper scooped him up and held him while he talked to the class. "Last time you were here, you got to see some of the farm. Today, we'll finish the tour in one big group. Kathleen and Tom can help me answer your questions."

"When will we get to do our projects?"

Danny asked, holding up an empty coffee can and a spade. He planned to dig up a sample of Mr. P.'s soil and one from back home and test them both with this little kit that told whether they were acid or base. Then he was going to plant a bean in each type of soil and see whether the plants that grew would be any different. Jonathan and his friends had started calling him Dirty Dan.

"After we're finished looking around, you'll have some time to work on your projects," Mr. Popper replied. "Follow me."

I took my camera out of its case (I'd loaded it on the bus) so I could take pictures while Mr. P. showed us around. Kathleen tugged my ponytail hello. I snapped a picture of her. On our way to the barn, I took pictures of Wilbur and Domino, asleep as usual. Red hopped up on the fence around their pen and scolded me. It seemed like a good time to get a picture of him, too, so I edged forward and snapped. He leaped off the fence straight at me!

"Hey, Red! Back up on the fence!" Mr. Popper ordered, getting between me and the bird. Red squawked angrily, but he obeyed.

In the barn—phew, what a smell! On one side there were two horses, a big coffee-colored one and a smaller one that was light but-

terscotch. Kathleen went over and scratched their faces. On the other side, two cows flicked their tails and chewed their cud.

Tom sat down on a stool next to one of the cows. "We still do our milking by hand here, but on dairy farms where they have a lot of cows, it's all done by machine." He pulled one of the finger-like teats on the cow's udder and a stream of milk squirted into a pail. "Anyone want to try?" he asked.

Lots of hands went up, including mine, but Tom picked Paul. He got milk out on the first try, although it squirted onto his sneakers. "Looks like you need a little help with your aim." Tom laughed.

"At least if you get thirsty, you can suck on your sneakers," Jonathan said. We all laughed, even Paul. I took a picture of Tom, Paul, and the cow.

Then Mr. Popper took us over to the henhouse to see his big incubator. "Time to get yours going now, Jonathan," he said.

Jonathan turned on a switch connected to his battery pack. Then he opened the box and checked inside. The light bulb was on. This time I took a picture for real.

Mr. Popper's incubator looked like a tall cabinet with drawers full of eggs. He explained that he wrote dates on the drawers to keep track of when the different groups of eggs were due to hatch. He opened a drawer labeled September 23 and selected one for Jonathan.

"It takes about three weeks for a chicken egg to hatch," he told us. "This egg is already ten days old." He handed Jonathan the egg. "Try to hold your portable incubator steady so the egg doesn't roll around too much."

Jonathan put the egg carefully inside. "Make yourself at home, Fred," he said to it.

It was hard to believe that Fred the egg would ever become a fluffy little chick like the new babies Mr. P. kept in a special heated area. Mr. Popper picked up two of the little peepers and gave us all a chance to hold them. When he put one in my hand, it felt as light as a marshmallow. Its tiny feet tickled my palm.

After the chicks, we went outside to the goats. Mr. Popper had sixteen. "On this farm, we specialize in making cheese from goat's milk," he told us. "We sell it to fine restaurants and shops. Goat cheese is considered a real delicacy."

Kathleen brought out some wedges of the caramel-brown cheese for us to try.

"Oooh, it smells like dirty socks!" Lisa complained. But Kathleen was munching some, and she looked as if she liked it, so I closed my eyes and took a bite.

"How is it?" Lisa asked.

"I think I'm going to throw up," I answered.

"You're welcome to go into the goat pen," Mr. Popper said. "The goats are very gentle unless they're annoyed. Just remember to close and latch the gate behind you."

The goats were as curious as babies. They tried to put everything in their mouths: my camera, Lisa's shopping bags, our shoelaces. As I petted a cute brown-and-white goat, I felt a tug at my ponytail. I spun around expecting it to be Kathleen again, but instead a big tan goat stood there smiling his funny goat smile.

"Oh no!" I reached around and felt my hair. Too late. It was damp and probably smelly.

After a few minutes, Mr. Popper called us. We slipped through the gate one at a time, careful to keep the goats from following us out.

"Now you will have about an hour to work on your projects," he said. "Those of you who don't need help may wander around on your own. We'll meet for lunch at twelve o'clock at the tables in the apple orchard. People who need help, come talk with Kathleen, Tom, or me over by the barn."

Lisa had to meet with Mr. Popper to find out what she would be allowed to take home for her cooking project. "I hope he doesn't make me use that disgusting cheese," she said, as she walked away.

I thought some goat pictures would add humor to my report, so I slipped inside the pen and made sure to latch the gate. I pulled my baseball cap out of my bag and put it on one of the goats' horns. The goat did look pretty funny. But when it tilted its head up and stretched out its tongue toward the cap, I had to distract it with a piece of sliced apple I'd brought along. While it chomped away, I looked through my camera lens, scanning for the best angle.

What I saw made me furious. Jonathan Adler! He had sneaked into the pen and had his incubator in one hand and *my sweatshirt* in the other. He must have taken it right out of my tote bag! Gingerly, he rested his incubator on a corner fence post and started waving my shirt at one of the goats. The goat trotted over and licked a sleeve.

"Jonathan! Give me that!" I shouted.

But Jonathan just laughed. "Why don't you take another picture, Mandy? Or isn't your camera loaded now?" He dangled the sleeve in the goat's face. The goat decided this was a game. It caught the sleeve in its mouth and began a little tug-of-war.

I balanced my camera on top of the nearest fence post, then ran over and grabbed my shirt. Jonathan dropped his end, but the goat didn't want to let go.

"Shoo!" I shouted. "Drop it!"

The goat just stared at me with my shirt clamped in its mouth. Jonathan cackled hysterically.

"You'd better get my sweatshirt back, or you're going to have to get me a new one!" I warned him.

"Aw, why don't you let him have it? It looks a lot better on him than it does on you."

"Oh yeah? I bet Mr. Popper won't think so." I headed toward the gate.

"Mandy, wait! I'll get your dumb sweatshirt," Jonathan called. He caught a sleeve and pulled. "Let go!" he commanded.

The goat pulled back, shaking its head from side to side.

"That's really great, Jonathan. He sure is

listening to you." I was almost enjoying this.

Jonathan scowled and pulled harder. "I said drop it, you turkey!"

"You're the turkey. He's a goat."

That did it; Jonathan was furious. He held on tight to my shirt and shoved the goat away.

Boy, did that make the goat angry! In an instant, it had jerked the sweatshirt out of Jonathan's hand and put its head down so its horns pointed right at us.

"Uh-oh," Jonathan said. "I think we'd better get out of here!"

I ran to the gate, unlatched it, and slipped through. But Jonathan stopped to get his incubator. With his back to the goat, he made a perfect target.

"Look out!" I screamed.

Jonathan whirled around, but the goat's head caught him right in the stomach. When he hit the ground, the incubator lid popped open and the egg bounced out. It landed without a sound, its shell cracked to pieces. A puddle of milky liquid and blood oozed into the dirt.

"Oh no!" I gasped.

"Fred!" Jonathan wailed.

Murderer!

I went back into the pen. Jonathan was kneeling, staring at the broken egg. Inside the mess, you could actually see the beginnings of the chick's tiny body. Its head was the size of a pea, with a dark spot that was the beginning of an eye. Its skin was so thin, you could see blood vessels underneath.

Suddenly Jonathan looked up at me. "It's all your fault, Mandy. You pushed that goat. You're a murderer!"

"I am not! You started all this!" I shouted back. Hot tears welled up in my eyes. I wasn't a murderer! This was just as much his fault as it was mine. I looked at the bloody puddle and thought about the chicks we'd played with in the barn. It was hard not to cry.

A lot of kids had come running over, and they stood outside the pen and gaped. "Oh gross! Chicken soup!" Matt exclaimed.

"What's going on here?" Mr. Popper asked from behind me. He glanced down at Fred. "You two stay here," he said. "The rest of you go back to your projects." Lisa gave me a sympathetic look as she walked away.

Mr. Popper turned to Jonathan and me. "What's going on here? I brought this class to my farm because I thought I could trust all of you to behave like thoughtful, dependable people, but you've really disappointed me." He looked down at the broken egg. "You know, on a farm, animals are born and die each day. But we never waste life unnecessarily, like this."

"But Mr. Popper, I didn't mean . . ."

"It doesn't matter what you meant, Amanda, it's how you behaved. Both of you. This trip to my farm is a special privilege. You haven't treated it that way. I don't really care which one of you started this trouble; I just don't want to see anything like it happen again—ever.

"Now, on the way home, you will have to share a seat without creating any disturbance. Otherwise, in the future, you will alternate going on class trips. And that would mean you'd each miss half. Consider yourselves lucky that you're getting a second chance. This chick didn't."

Before I could think of anything to say, he left the pen.

Jonathan glared at me again and ran after him.

So many feelings were jumbled up inside me. I was really mad at Jonathan, but I was mad at myself, too. It had been sort of fun fighting with the goat and Jonathan—before the goat got angry. But I never would have tangled with the goat—or with Jonathan—if I had known it would have put Fred in danger.

How could I explain it all to Mr. Popper? If Jonathan hadn't taken my sweatshirt, none of this would have happened. But maybe I had started it by tricking him at the bus. It looked like I was flunking self-control pretty badly.

I stood alone in the pen, lost in thought. The goats just ignored me. My tote bag was still propped up against the fence, and my sweatshirt and baseball cap lay in the dust near the remains of poor Fred. I picked them up and walked over to the fence post where I'd placed my camera. It was nowhere in sight.

I looked on all the other fence posts. I looked around the feed and water troughs. Had Jonathan taken my camera without my noticing? As I wondered where it could be, something caught my eye down in the goats' big water trough. I looked more closely. There was my camera, at the very bottom. The angry goat must have knocked it off the fence post when I raced out of the pen.

As I bent down and reached into the water, a goat nuzzled my neck. Suddenly I wished I could be a goat, too. My camera was ruined, my film was ruined, my project was ruined— my whole life was ruined!

When I stood up, Mr. Popper was beside me. He saw my dripping camera and put his arm around me.

"Oh Mr. Popper, I'm sorry," I cried. "Nothing's gone right. I even killed my camera."

"You're just a good kid having a bad day," he said. "I know you won't get into trouble like this again. Go have lunch with the class. You'll feel better after you've eaten."

I walked over to where Lisa was sitting with Lacey and Sarah, and I plopped down next to her. I wasn't hungry. "My camera's been swimming in the goats' water trough," I announced miserably.

"Oh, Mandy, your camera! Can it be fixed?" Lisa asked.

"I doubt it. And my film is definitely drowned. Now I can't even do my project."

"You can share mine," Lisa said. "We can ask Mr. P. if we can cook together."

"I still want to do something on my own." I sighed. "But thanks for offering."

"I'll try to help you think of something on the way home."

Lisa was trying to cheer me up, but it only made me feel worse. "Mr. P. is making Jonathan and me ride home together."

"You have to sit with Jonathan for two hours? Oh, poor you!"

Poor me was right! When I got on the bus, Jonathan was already planted behind Mr. Popper, reading a book about Bigfoot, pretending not to notice me. His incubator was next to him, leaving me just a small space.

"Be careful," he hissed, as I wriggled in. He placed the incubator on his lap protectively. "You're not getting another chance to murder a chick."

"He gave you *another* egg?" I couldn't believe it! Had Mr. Popper told Jonathan that he was just a good kid having a bad day, too? Couldn't he see that every day was a bad day with Jonathan?

"Mr. P. knows *I* can act responsibly," Jonathan boasted.

I took out my copy of *So You Want to Be a Reporter?* and pretended to read, so I wouldn't have to look at him. But there was nothing in the book about what to do if your film got soaked. My project was ruined, but Jonathan's was saved. It just wasn't fair.

After dinner that night, I went upstairs to mope around. Tammy was lying on the floor of her room, coloring. "Want to see my cats?" she asked.

"Sure." She had about twenty cat drawings scattered around her.

"I'd let you use my camera, if I had one," she said, drawing a big red smile on a pink cat.

"Thanks. But even if you had one, my project would still be ruined. The trip's over, and my film is destroyed. You can't make a photo journal without photographs."

Tammy picked up a purple crayon and began to color stripes on one of her cats' tails. "Draw it," she said.

"Come on, Tammy, I can't draw that whole farm."

"Just draw the hilarious parts," she insisted, using her favorite vocabulary word.

"Tammy, I don't think you understand. This wasn't funny." But then I thought about Paul squirting milk on his sneaker, the goat eating my ponytail, and Jonathan getting butted in the stomach.

"Tammy, you know that new pack of pastel paper I've been saving?"

"You mean the one you told me not to touch?"

"I'm going to open it now. And you can use as much as you want."

The
Project Blues

Mr. Popper gave us four weeks to complete our projects. We were supposed to do most of the work at home, but there was also a project period on Wednesdays and Fridays after lunch. During the first week, we mostly read our books and took notes, but after that, the class began painting, drawing, building, and growing.

During one of those Friday periods, our principal, Dr. Hutch, visited the classroom. "Well, you all look busy," she boomed, as we looked up from our work. Dr. Hutch is about six feet tall and has a big, deep voice.

"They're working on their independent study projects," Mr. Popper explained. "We've got quite an interesting bunch this year."

"Wonderful!" She walked over to a movable chalkboard where Mr. Popper had written down all the projects with our names next to them.

"'A Scarecrow,'" she read out loud. "What a fabulous idea! 'The World's Largest Indoor Tomato.' Marvelous!" Dr. Hutch clasped her hands to her chest with enthusiasm. "'How Earthworms Help Our Soil.' Fascinating! 'Pig Sense.' Spectacular!" She clapped a hand on either side of her face like she was ecstatic. "'A Day in the Life of a Farmer.' Excellent! 'How to Make Cheese from Goat's Milk.' Extraordinary!" She put a hand over her heart. I was afraid she was going to drop dead with joy.

"You know, boys and girls"—she turned to the class—"these projects sound so interesting, I think you should share them with the rest of the school. Perhaps we could hold a project fair in your classroom. What do you think, Mr. Popper?"

"Oh, I think we could do something like that, don't you, kids?"

You bet we did!

"Let's have the fair in the afternoon on the day the projects are due," Mr. Popper said.

"That way we'll have the morning to set up. You kids had better get busy. The fair is less than three weeks away!"

I was using up a lot of paper and markers, but my drawings of chickens still looked like dinosaurs and my goats still looked like dogs. One afternoon, when I was trying to draw Kathleen eating goat cheese, Tammy came into my room.

"What's that?" she asked, peering over my shoulder.

"What does it look like?"

"A girl screaming."

"Thanks a lot, Tam. It's supposed to be a girl eating."

"Then I guess she doesn't like how it tastes," Tammy said, thoughtfully. Before she could say anything else, the phone rang.

"It's Lisa," Mom shouted.

"Hi," said Lisa, when I picked up. Her voice was flat.

"What's wrong?"

"I just made an apple pie. I was going to freeze it until our projects were due. . . ."

"How is it?"

"Not too good. The apples all turned to juice. There are hardly any chunks left. And the crust is so wet, it's just swimming in the pie pan."

"That's too bad," I sympathized. But inside, I felt a twinge of relief. I was glad I wasn't the only one with the project blues. "My chickens look like miniature dinosaurs," I confessed.

"Really?" She sounded almost pleased. "Our projects will be on display for the whole school. It's going to be so embarrassing!"

"Don't remind me. We'd better get back to work."

Two minutes later, the phone rang again. It was Lisa. "Guess what I just heard on the radio!" Her voice was definitely perkier. "Wishman Rocker is going to give a concert here in Hartman on the Saturday after Thanksgiving! The ad says he's coming home for the holidays. And he's going to grant three wishes at the concert!"

Wishman Rocker was my favorite rock musician. I played his tape, *Wish Upon a Rock Star* all the time. He actually grew up in our town. His name was Ronald Flugelman then. He was the only star I'd heard of who came from Hartman. Wishman's trademark was his make-a-wish contest. At each concert, everyone in the audience wrote down a wish, and he'd pick out a few and grant them.

"I'd love to see him! Maybe your father could take us," I suggested. Since her parents' divorce, her father often took her places like skiing and the circus, when he came to visit. My mother once wrote an article about divorced fathers who treated every visiting day as though it were their kid's birthday. She called them Disneyland Dads.

It got so quiet on the other end of the phone, I thought maybe we'd been disconnected. Then Lisa said, "He won't be here. His company is sending him to work on a special project in Japan. He's leaving this weekend." Her voice shook a little.

"Japan! For how long?"

"I'm not sure. Maybe a year. He's going to be there all summer. Maybe I won't get to see him for a whole year!"

"Of course you will!" I exclaimed. "Your dad couldn't stand being away from you that long! He'll probably mail you a plane ticket soon. In fact, you should be getting ready for the trip by learning about Japanese culture and stuff. Remember that report I did on Japan last year?"

"Sure."

"I still have all the pamphlets I got from Molson's Travel Agency. You can have them."

"Okay." She paused. "Mandy, don't tell anyone about my father going to Japan. Not even Lacey or Sarah."

"Why not?"

"It's embarrassing to have everyone think your father doesn't care about you."

"He cares, Lisa. I know he cares." I tried to think of something to cheer her up. "Listen, maybe my dad will take us to the concert."

"I guess that would be okay." But she didn't sound very enthusiastic. "Are your chickens coming out any better?"

"No, but I haven't given up yet. I'll talk to you later." I hung up and went back upstairs to try again.

In school the next day, Mr. P. was absent. Our substitute was a very short woman about my grandmother's age, who told us her name was Mrs. Pressman. "I've written the page numbers of the assignments Mr. Popper left for you on the board," she said, cheerfully. "He told me to have you work on your independent study projects when you're through."

First, I put our vocabulary words into sentences. Then, although I'm great at division, I did the problems slowly and checked each one. I wasn't very anxious to get to my project.

My drawings still looked ridiculous. Finally, when I couldn't stall any longer, I took out some markers and paper.

Lisa finished her math and language too. "Great," she said, pursing her mouth in a silly grin, "I'll just cook right here at my desk."

"I almost forgot! I brought my stuff on Japan for you. You can look at it." I got up from my desk and went to the closet at the back of the classroom where my book bag was.

Jonathan was back there, too, poking around in his jacket. He was so intent on finding whatever it was he wanted, he didn't notice me. I groped in my bag for the brochures. We both found what we wanted at the same time— I pulled out the Japan pamphlets and he pulled out a fistful of cap bombs, *which absolutely were not allowed at school, not even in the yard!*

"You're not going to use those in here, are you?" I hissed. "You'll give Mrs. Pressman a heart attack!" They make a lot of noise and smoke when you toss them on the ground.

Jonathan just smirked.

"You'd better not! Dr. Hutch will come in here and punish the whole class," I warned him.

"Young man, young lady, just what is going

on back there?" Mrs. Pressman made her way to the back of the room.

"Quick, take these," I said, thrusting the brochures at Jonathan to cover up his handful of bombs. "I'm just showing him these pamphlets," I told Mrs. Pressman, as she stood in front of us. She was the only teacher I'd ever had who was my height.

She glanced at the booklets in Jonathan's fist."*Touring Tokyo.* It's nice to see young people so interested in learning about the world."

"I really want to go there some day. I did a report about Japan last year," I babbled. "Did you know that it's actually made up of thousands of islands, but the whole country is smaller than California?"

"Very nice, dear, but I'm afraid you two will have to sit down now. Perhaps you could continue your discussion at lunch."

"Sure," Jonathan agreed, smiling like an angel.

As soon as Mrs. Pressman turned her back, I snatched my brochures from Jonathan. "Cone head! You're lucky I saved your neck." I brushed by him toward my desk.

"Sayonara," he jeered.

But out of the corner of my eye, I saw him drop the cap bombs back in his book bag.

Just one week before project day, I awoke at 2 A.M. and stared into the darkness. In seven days my journal would be on display for the entire school to see, and I still hadn't drawn any decent pictures. Like a fish on a dock, I flopped around in bed for a while. Finally I got up, turned on the light, and looked over my bookshelf for something to read. Even though I loved *From the Mixed-Up Files of Mrs. Basil E. Frankweiler,* I decided it might give me nightmares; I passed up *Julie of the Wolves* for the same reason; and I didn't feel much like laughing at *Where the Sidewalk Ends.* The next book I came to was *Cartooning for Kids.*

I pulled it off the shelf and flipped through the pages of cats with mouths like upside-down umbrellas and people with question marks for noses. Suddenly, just like in a cartoon, a light bulb went on in my head. Why hadn't I thought of it before? My pictures didn't have to look real. I could draw cartoons instead! My project could be a comic-book journal.

I began reading the instructions for drawing goats, but I was already feeling sleepy. I slipped the book under my bed and shut off the light. Tomorrow I'd start over.

The
Five-Dollar Word

When project day finally arrived, I followed a trail of straw down the hall and up to the door of our classroom. Standing guard outside was Stacey's scarecrow, dressed as a punk rocker. It had blue cotton hair, one dangly rhinestone earring, purple sunglasses, a sweatshirt that said I HATE CROWS!, a pair of blue jeans, and two different sneakers. In its arms it held a sign that said WELCOME TO THE PROJECT FAIR, with an arrow pointing into the classroom.

"He's fantastic, Stacey!" I said, giving her a handful of straw.

She stuffed it back under his shirt. "Thanks, Mandy. Wait till you see the others!"

Desks and chairs had been moved out of the

way, and the room was ringed by long tables. Lacey and Sarah were taping up posters explaining their projects. I found Lisa setting out trays of food she'd prepared. Each tray had a label that told the name of the dish and its ingredients: Apple Crumble, Fried Zucchini, Goat-Cheese Fritters, and Hard-Boiled Eggs. In the center was a basket of Puffy Popovers.

"Lisa, this looks incredible!" I gasped. "You could open a restaurant."

Her mouth tightened in an embarrassed little smile. "My mother helped a lot. Too much. She thinks everything has to be perfect all the time. Just don't try the goat-cheese fritters. They're really awful."

I wandered over to where Lacey was tying a bow around a droopy little plant. In front of it a sign read: WATCH THE WORLD'S LARGEST INDOOR TOMATO GROWING!

"Where's the tomato?" I asked.

"What do you think this is?" She pointed to a single green ball—about the size of a marble—hanging from a thin stem.

"This is the world's largest indoor tomato?"

"Careful or you'll hurt its feelings; tomato plants are very sensitive," she whispered. Then she spoke louder so the tomato could hear. "This tomato gets fed every other day.

I've planted it in the richest kind of potting soil. It gets all the sun that's available *and* it has a grow-light, too. I water it as soon as it's dry. I even talk to it." She looked at the plant and shook her finger at it. "And if it doesn't start growing bigger soon, I'm going to make spaghetti sauce out of it!"

There was a commotion over in the back corner of the room where Jonathan was standing. One day in class, he'd announced that his egg had hatched, but we'd only seen snapshots of the egg cracking and the damp, ugly baby bird that it had produced. Half the class was pushing and shoving to see it. Now I decided to give in to my curiosity and went over to join the group.

"Look out! Here comes killer Mandy." Matthew stood aside in mock horror.

I brushed by him and squeezed up to the table. Jonathan had his chick in a glass tank topped with chicken wire. The chick still had fuzzy yellow feathers and hopped around on clumsy baby legs, but it was bigger than the ones that Mr. P. had shown us. Jonathan had taped a sign to the glass that said RED JUNIOR.

The chick was so adorably goofy, I forgot for a moment that I hated Jonathan. "Could I hold him?" I asked.

"You think I'd actually let a chick murderer hold Red Junior?" he sneered.

Angrily, I walked away. But it wasn't so much Jonathan and his chick that were bothering me. I went over to the closet and opened my backpack. When I pulled out my journal, it felt lighter than a bag of potato chips. Everyone else had projects you could taste or touch or watch. How could I have thought that a comic-strip journal was such a great idea? Who came to a fair to read, anyway? No one. I tossed it onto one of the tables where it landed face up, with my cover of a rooster, a cow, and a goat all chasing a bunch of kids. My drawing had looked better at home.

We passed most of the morning looking at each other's projects and chatting. Lisa was the first person to read mine. "Mandy, this is really great!" she said, when she'd finished.

"You have to say that. You're my best friend."

"No, I mean it!"

Lacey took the journal from her and flipped through the pages. "What cute goats! Your cartoons are really good."

"Thanks." I figured she was just being polite, too. Lacey is a really terrific artist. She could have done a much better job.

They were the only two kids in the whole class who looked at it.

Mr. Popper dismissed us early for lunch. He said it was because we weren't in the right frame of mind to concentrate. "Just be ready to be good hosts to our visitors this afternoon," he reminded us.

After lunch, the kindergartners were the first to visit. Their teachers, Mrs. Bluestone and Miss Shelley, took them around the room in an orderly two-by-two line, except for Ralphie, the class troublemaker. Mrs. Bluestone held his hand. We stood behind the tables waiting for questions. Paul's earthworms were a big favorite.

"Earthworms help break down the soil. Their burrowing makes room for the air that plant roots need," Paul recited, as the kindergartners stared at the pale, naked worms squirming like a bunch of chopped-off pinkies.

"Sometimes I cut 'em in half," Ralphie told Paul, proudly.

Paul smiled at Ralphie. "Do you want to hold one?" he offered.

Ralphie pulled free of Mrs. Bluestone, and Paul dropped a wriggling worm into his palm. Ralphie stroked the worm as if it were a dog.

The kids continued around the room, examining projects. They all wanted to try milking Matthew's papier-mâché cow. Its udder spurted milk when you pushed a button on the end of an electrical cord coming out of the cow. They loved Lisa's popovers, but not even Ralphie would taste a goat-cheese fritter. I stood behind the table where my journal was displayed. The kids breezed right by me to Jonathan's chick. They didn't even look at my project. I didn't blame them, though. I probably would have done the same.

They all listened attentively while Jonathan explained how he'd hatched Red Junior—all except for Ralphie, that is. Ralphie was busy dangling Paul's worm through the chicken-wire screen. The chick came forward to examine the offering. The poor worm tried to wiggle away, but in an instant the greedy chick snatched it out of Ralphie's fingers and almost swallowed it whole.

"Ralphie!" scolded Mrs. Bluestone, when she realized what had happened. The chick's throat was so short that half the worm hung out its beak. Ralphie's classmates began to shriek.

"My worm!" exclaimed Paul. He rushed over to the tank.

"Hey! He'll choke!" Jonathan shouted, when he saw Red Junior struggling. He pulled up the screen and grabbed the worm. But the chick clamped its beak shut.

Jonathan tugged, the chick bit—and the worm split in two. The kindergartners murmured appreciatively. Red Junior swallowed his end. Jonathan handed the other end over to Paul. "I owe you half a worm," he said.

"I think it's time for us to go," Mrs. Bluestone told Mr. Popper. And with Ralphie firmly in tow, she marched the kindergartners out of the room.

The first graders—the next group of visitors—were already lined up outside our door. I saw Tammy peeking out from behind her teacher, Mrs. Rodriguez, and I waved. She gave me a big jack-o'-lantern grin.

Mrs. Rodriguez let her class walk around the room by themselves while she chatted with Mr. Popper. Little groups of kids bunched up in front of Paul's worms, Jonathan's chick, Lacey's tomato, Danny's beans, Matthew's cow, Yuki's diorama, and the other projects, too. But nobody came to look at mine.

I watched Tammy make a strangely slow

trip around the room. I could tell she really wasn't looking at the projects. But she wouldn't turn to look at me, either. Finally, after passing by everything else, she had worked her way over to my side of the display tables.

"Hi," I said.

She didn't answer me. In fact, she acted like she didn't even know me. She picked up my journal and began to read.

"Ha, ha, ha, ha, HA! This is *hysterical!*" she said. She shook her best friend, Betsey, by the shoulder. "Look at this! Isn't it *hysterical?*"

"Yeah!" Betsey agreed, peering over Tammy's shoulder. "Look what the goat is doing!"

"What did you say?" Tammy roared, as though she were deaf.

"IT IS HYSTERICAL!" Betsey shouted.

Tammy and Betsey made a big show of laughing loudly over every single page.

"Tammy," I whispered, "stop acting crazy!"

But Tammy and Betsey kept giggling and guffawing, and soon lots of their classmates were pushing and tugging, trying to get hold of my project.

"Let me have it next!"

"No, I want it!"

"If you pass it to me first, I'll give you some gum!"

"Read it to me! I don't know what this word says!"

I couldn't believe what was happening! Mrs. Rodriguez had to come over and calm them down. "Perhaps we could have Amanda read it aloud to all of you," Mrs. Rodriguez suggested. "Would that be all right with you, Mr. Popper?"

Tammy had a big, dopey grin on her face. If we'd been alone, I would've kissed her.

I took my report from Tammy and waited for the kids to be quiet. Then I began reading:

Mandy's Journal of How Not to Act When Visiting a Farm

by Amanda Simon

If you're ever in Mr. Popper's fifth-grade class, you'll probably get to visit his farm. Or maybe someday you'll visit someone else's farm. If you do, there are a few things you'll need to know—like how to act. I'll tell you what some members of our class, including me, did when we visited last October. Then all you have to remember is not to act the same way.

71

You should never tease someone before going on a long ride—it gives them too much time to figure out how they're going to get you back!

Do not try to pet the rooster. Also, do not turn your back on the rooster. Especially if his name is Red, as in blood red.

If you're offered a chance to milk a cow, take your sneakers off first.

Mr. P. has two cows. When they're not giving milk, their main activity seems to be chewing. <u>Do</u> <u>not</u> <u>accept</u> <u>any</u> <u>gum</u> <u>from</u> <u>a</u> <u>cow</u>!

Be very careful in the henhouse, too. There are a lot of breakables inside. And whatever you do, don't stand in front of an egg while it's hatching. If you're the first thing the chick sees when it gets out, it will think you're its mother. This happened to Jonathan. He may be the only eleven-year-old boy in the world who is also a mother!

Goats will eat anything, but they especially like hair. I heard that the last group of kids that went into Mr. P.'s goat pen came out bald. You'd better wear a hat.

Mr. P. makes cheese out of goat's milk. You may be offered a taste. Don't sample any! As my friend Lisa says, it smells like dirty socks. It tastes like them, too.

Finally, no matter what, <u>never get into a fight with a goat</u>. Jonathan and I got into a fight with one of Mr. P.'s goats. It launched Jonathan into the air like a soccer ball. It launched my camera into its drinking water.

Worst of all, it launched a baby chick out of its shell before it was ready. That was sad.

When I was a little kid, I thought I might want to be a farmer. Now that I know better, I think maybe I'll be a tightrope walker in the circus. It's a lot safer up there.

THE END

How Not to Win
a Window-Painting
Contest

Things seemed awfully quiet for a whole week after the project fair. But the next Monday morning while Mr. P. was taking attendance, Dr. Hutch's voice came booming over the loudspeaker.

"Attention fifth and sixth graders! It's almost time for Hartman's Annual Holiday Window-Painting Contest, which will be held on the Saturday before Thanksgiving from 9 A.M. to noon. Contestants may paint individually or in teams of two. Your teachers all received a registration sheet this morning. Remember, only fifth and sixth graders may enter. If you wish to participate, please sign up by Friday."

There was a burst of applause from the

class. The window-painting contest was held every year, and we were finally old enough to enter!

"Hold it down," Mr. Popper said. "I'll post the registration sheet on the bulletin board, and you can all sign up right before lunch. The contest rules will be here on my desk. Don't forget to take one if you're going to participate."

Lacey raised her hand. "What are the prizes?"

Mr. Popper scanned the registration sheet. "Prizes include tickets for the winner or winners and their escort, who must be eighteen years of age or older, to the Wishman Rocker concert at the Hartman Music Hall . . ."

"Oh my God!" Lacey shrieked.

". . . gift certificates from Poppa's Pizza," Mr. P. continued reading, "and Wishman Rocker record albums."

Lisa and I stared at each other with our mouths open. Here was our chance!

It was a long wait until lunch. All I could think about was the contest. I put my decimal point in the wrong place on our math quiz, and during reading I lost my place in *Summer of the Swans*. I was almost eleven years old and I still hadn't been to a rock concert, but now maybe I could change that.

When lunchtime finally came, there was a rush to the bulletin board. Sarah and Lacey got there first. I felt my stomach do a little jump as I watched them sign up. Lacey is the best artist in the whole school. Once in a while, my drawings get picked to be in the display case outside the art room, but the art teacher *always* picks Lacey's. Her bus-safety poster of a kid and a bus shaking hands was still on display, even though Bus Safety Week had been over for months. Sarah is Lacey's best friend, and she's a pretty good artist, too.

"Look, it's girls only," Lisa said, nodding at the line behind us.

It was true. So far, only Stacey, Yuki, Danielle, and Rachel were there. But Jonathan, Paul, and Matthew were standing together at the back of the room eyeing the line and murmuring. If they joined, they'd be sure to find some way of ruining our chance. I held my breath until they headed for the school yard.

Lisa came home with me after school, so we could plan our painting. We went up to my room and I put on my Wishman Rocker tape. "Did you bring a copy of the rules?" I asked.

She pulled them out of her backpack.

" 'Each contestant or team of contestants will be assigned to paint a holiday scene on a window along Main Street. Entries will be judged on their originality, artistic quality, and neatness,' " she read. " 'Contestants must be prepared to leave the area where they are working completely free of litter and paint. *No paint spills are to be left behind.* ' "

Lisa looked around. "We'd better bring a lot of rags, Mandy, because we both know what a slob you are."

"Thanks a lot!" I took my pillow out from under my bed and threw it at her. "Actually it said in an article that my mom wrote for *Real Women* that slobbiness is a sign of creativity— and that's what we need to win."

"Then I guess my mother is the most un-creative person in the world," Lisa grumbled. "She gets crazy if our house isn't in perfect order. Not like my dad. He doesn't care whether I hang up my clothes or put away my books. In his apartment, he never even hangs up his own jacket." She stopped suddenly and looked away as if she were embarrassed. "We'd better get to work if we want to go to that concert."

I pulled my drawing pad out from under my

bed. Then I fished under there for a pencil.

We looked at each other for a minute, wondering where to start. "Maybe we should brainstorm," I suggested. "I'll make a list: pilgrims . . . turkeys . . . Indians . . ."

"Snow . . . Christmas trees . . . Santa . . . sleds," Lisa added.

"Menorahs . . . candles . . . presents," I continued.

"Candy canes . . . snowballs . . . snowmen . . . skis . . ."

"Lisa, wait! I think you've got something," I interrupted. "Snowmen could be great."

"Why?"

"Because they're easy to draw. Just three circles and a top hat."

Lisa saw the practicality of this right away. "Okay. Let's try."

We drew a lot of pictures of snowmen doing snowy things like sledding and skiing. Finally we came up with an idea we both loved. It was a scene of snowmen dancing in a circle under a full moon. The sky would be black with lots of twinkling stars that would spell out Peace on Earth. It would be beautiful!

"Wishman Rocker, here we come!" Lisa crossed her fingers and looked heavenward.

"I wish on your granny! I wish on your auntie! I wish on your plant-y! That you'd wear something scanty!" Wishman wailed on my tape. His songs were a lot better if you didn't listen too hard to the words.

When painting day finally came, Mom drove Tammy and me down to Main Street where the contest was held. Tammy was going to be our gofer. A gofer is a person who "goes for" things for other people. Sort of like a servant. I learned in Mom's article "How Real Women Make Movies" that there are people on movie sets who actually have that job. Mom says having a gofer is a little like having a wife.

Tammy bounced up and down in the back seat all the way into the village. I was excited, too, but mostly I felt nervous.

We were assigned to paint the window at Wilson's World of Toys. It was one of the best locations, right in the middle of Main Street. Lisa and her mom got there at the same time we did.

"Are you sure you have everything you need?" Mrs. Krauss asked us.

"I think so," I answered, gazing at our two bulgy bags of paint, brushes, rags, newspaper, and other supplies.

"I already told you we did, Mom." Lisa's voice was irritable.

Mr. Wilson came out of his store. "Good morning, girls." He patted Tammy on the head. "Are you their helper?"

"I'm their gofer."

"A gopher? Where's your tail? You look like a little girl to me."

"Not that kind." Tammy giggled. "I have to change the water and wash their brushes."

"Well, come in and use the bathroom in the back of the store anytime you want," Mr. Wilson offered.

Mom gave me a kiss. "Good luck! Daddy will pick you up later." She turned to Mrs. Krauss. "Do you want Ron to bring Lisa home, too?"

"If it's not too much trouble." Lisa's mother put an arm around Lisa. "Be careful, honey."

"Of what?" Lisa asked, impatiently.

Mrs. Krauss looked hurt. "Nothing. Have fun."

"I'll go into the toy store and fill up your water jar," Tammy volunteered. She skipped inside with the jar.

We spread out newspapers below the window and taped them down. Then we started by outlining the snowmen in black paint. But painting on a window is a lot different than painting on paper. My brush skidded and slid along the glass. The paint kept running and smudging and I had to keep mopping up the drips. "This was easier to do at home," I complained.

"We did it with pencils and paper at home," Lisa reminded me. "I guess we should have practiced painting it."

"This water's black already," Tammy chirped. "I'll go change it."

Lisa stood back and examined our outlining. "Our snowmen looked better in the sketch."

"I know. Now they look more like clowns." I pointed my brush at a snowman I'd painted, with a too-big smile. "Especially this one."

"Well, let's start adding some color. Maybe that will help."

I leaned over to wash the black paint off my brush, but the water jar was gone. "Where's Tammy?"

"Here I am," she called, coming out of the toy store. "You should see the gymnast doll in there!"

"Try to keep your mind on your job," I told her. "You're slowing us up. We need to have the clean water quickly."

"My birthday's coming soon, and I have to plan my wish list. Besides, it's boring standing here," she whined.

"Tammy, you just got here! Open a jar of white and mix it up for me. I'll paint some snow."

Tammy stirred up the paint as if she were mixing cake batter. "Oooh, oooh, gooey, gloppy, oooh, oooh, gooey, gloppy," she chanted. When the paint was smooth, she poked around in the shopping bags until she found an old dish towel Mom had given me for a rag. She tied it on her head like a kerchief. "I'm Goldilocks going to Grandma's," she sang, skipping around in circles.

I tried hard to ignore her.

"Oh Toto," Tammy said, petting an imaginary dog. "Do you think we'll meet a big, bad wolfie? We'd better hide inside this store." She held up our jar of water. "This water's all black again. Toto and I will change it for you." Goldilocks disappeared inside the store.

"Come back soon," I called after her. "And Toto's from the *Wizard of Oz,*" I couldn't help adding.

"I'll start painting the stars now," Lisa said. "The yellow should look nice against the black sky." As she worked, a drip of her yellow ran into my white.

Tammy and the water jar were still gone. I looked through the window. There she was, holding a doll in a leotard. I tapped on the glass.

She put the doll down and came to the door. "I need water, Tammy," I said. "Now!"

"You don't have to be so bossy! I left it in the bathroom. I have to go back there and get it."

What ever gave me the dumb idea that having Tammy around would be a help? "You're supposed to be helping, not playing!" I snapped, when she finally came back with the water. "Next time, don't stop to look at anything."

"If you're going to yell at me, I'm quitting."

"All right." I sighed. "I'm hungry. How about going to the bakery and getting us all some doughnuts to eat?"

Tammy's face brightened.

I pulled a dollar out of my pocket for her. "I'll have chocolate cream."

"Me too." Lisa handed her two quarters, and Tammy skipped off down the street.

Lisa and I surveyed the window. Our snowmen still looked like soccer balls with clown faces, but the yellow stars twinkled nicely against the black sky.

"It needs more color," Lisa said. "I'll make their boots red. At least we were able to get rid of those smudges. I think it looks pretty good so far."

I thought so, too. When Tammy came back with the doughnuts, we sat down on the sidewalk in front of our window to eat. Up and down Main Street, other groups of kids were also taking a break.

"Stacey and Rachel are painting the bakery window," Tammy reported, with jelly at the corners of her mouth.

"Use your napkin. What are they painting?"

"A Christmas tree made out of cupcakes and cookies. It's cute." She wiped her face with her sleeve.

I popped the last bite of doughnut into my mouth. "Let's go see how Lacey and Sarah are doing. They're painting the pharmacy window."

"Well, just for a minute," Lisa agreed. "We need to finish."

When we stood up, Tammy started to follow us. "You stay here and guard our window, Tammy," I told her.

"I want to come, too."

"It's just for two minutes. When we come back, you can go into the toy store."

Reluctantly, she sat back down.

When we got to the pharmacy, I almost wished we hadn't come. Lacey and Sarah's painting was gorgeous! It was a scene of chipmunks and birds at an ice skating party. They had cute little hats and mittens on and were gliding and tumbling on a pond surrounded by frosted pine trees. The chipmunks were reddish brown, and the birds were blue. Their hats and mittens were all sorts of bright colors, too. The painting was so cheerful I hated it.

"Hi Lacey, hi Sarah! How are you doing?" I asked, ignoring their window.

"My fingers have cramps," Lacey complained.

"We've used up most of our paint," Sarah added. "It's a good thing we're almost done."

I knew they were waiting for us to say something about their painting. "Your painting looks nice," I said casually. "Did you get the idea from the Alvin comics?"

"No," Lacey said. She looked surprised.

"Really? Well, your chipmunks look a lot

like the Alvin ones. I hope the judges don't think you copied them."

"I didn't!" Her voice was unnaturally high.

"I believe you. But I hear the judges are pretty strict about originality."

"I never even thought of Alvin," Sarah moaned.

"Well, don't worry," I said. "They probably won't notice. We've got to get back and finish. See you later. C'mon, Lisa."

Lisa gave me a funny look. She didn't move. "I think your painting is wonderful! It doesn't look anything like the Alvin comics to me. It's better! I wish ours had more color."

But her attempt to cheer them up didn't work. Neither Lacey nor Sarah were smiling.

I didn't wait for Lisa. Her niceness could be really annoying. She never acted like she cared about winning anything, whether it was a card game or a contest. I almost wished I was painting with someone else.

"Mandy, you said you'd only be gone two minutes!" Tammy groused, when I got back to Wilson's.

"Will you shut up! I'm tired of your complaining!" I shouted.

Tammy's face crumpled like a tissue and she

started crying. I felt like Paul's half a worm. "Look, I'm sorry," I said. "This contest has got me pretty nervous."

But she only cried louder.

"Tammy," I pleaded, "go into the toy store and look around. It'll make you feel better. *Please.*"

Tammy stopped sobbing, although her little shoulders continued to heave. She rubbed her eyes and walked off dejectedly, without speaking to me.

Lisa came back to paint, but we didn't talk, either. I knew she was mad at how I'd acted. Nothing was going right! Painting the window was a lot harder than I'd expected, Tammy was at her peskiest and I'd blown up at her, I'd been snotty to Lacey and Sarah, and now my best friend was fed up with me. It was my turn to feel like crying.

Silently, I finished the snowmen's red boots and Lisa gave them striped scarves. We put a few birds in the trees. When we were almost through, I stepped back for a good look. "Lisa! Come and see! Our window looks really good! It looks great!"

She put down her brush and came back to where I stood. "It does, it really does!"

Tammy came out of the store and joined us. "Mr. Wilson has a ring toss set in the shape of . . . Oh! The window looks so pretty!"

"Thanks." And I meant it. I was glad that she was talking to me again.

"Let's just add a little more snow to the branches of this tree," Lisa suggested.

"Okay." But as I turned to get some more white paint, I saw someone coming up the street that made me worry all over again.

Spills,
Chills, and Thrills

"What a stupid painting," jeered a familiar voice behind me. I began adding snowflakes and didn't answer. It was Jonathan.

"Are you deaf or just dumb?" he tried again. "I said your painting's stupid."

"So are you. Go bother someone else," I hissed.

"I think your stupid painting needs a little help, Mandy," he taunted, picking up one of my brushes and dipping it in the jar of black paint.

I dipped my paintbrush in black paint, too, and pointed it at him. "Leave our window alone or I'll help you paint your jacket. Or your face."

But my threat only seemed to make things

worse. Paintbrush dripping, Jonathan walked right up to our window. I reached out and gave him a shove. As he stumbled backward, he lost his balance and his foot kicked over the jars of paint that we'd lined up below the window.

Lisa and I watched in horror as paint ran all over the sidewalk. The blue jar rolled across the pavement and off the curb, then shattered into pieces.

Jonathan looked down, surprised. "Gee, Mandy, I didn't really mean to . . ."

But Lisa and I weren't listening. We were too busy picking up glass and sopping up the paint with rags and newspapers.

"Tammy! Go get more water and see if Mr. Wilson will lend us a broom and a dustpan," I ordered.

"What a disaster!" Lisa wailed. She reached for the yellow jar, which had stopped right at Jonathan's foot. He seemed frozen to the pavement. "Move, you idiot!" Lisa exploded. He ran off down the street. Lisa looked surprised.

A yellow Volkswagen pulled up at the curb. "Look out!" I shouted, just as its tire rolled over the broken glass. There was a loud pop like a giant balloon bursting.

"Oh no!" Lisa gasped.

Dr. Hutch got out of her car, walked around to the passenger side, and pulled a large shard of glass out from under the front tire. Her angry gaze followed the paint smears from the gutter to the sidewalk. "Mandy! Lisa!" she exploded. "Look at my tire! And this mess!"

"It wasn't our fault!" I began. "I had to push . . . I mean, I thought Jonathan was going to . . . That is, I didn't realize. . . ." I stopped. How could I explain? If I told on Jonathan, I'd have to admit I pushed him. Besides, he'd taken off right before Dr. Hutch arrived. It might look as if I were making the whole thing up. Lisa must have felt the same way. She didn't even try to explain.

"You know the rules of the contest," Dr. Hutch said, ignoring my babbling. "If you can't get the sidewalk cleaned up properly, you'll have to be penalized. I'm a member of the judging committee, and I expect to see you do a good job. Otherwise, you'll be disqualified."

"We'll get the sidewalk cleaned up perfectly," Lisa promised.

"I certainly hope so. But my tire is ruined. I'll have to arrange to have it fixed." Dr. Hutch turned and walked toward Bob's Garage.

I stared at the paint-splattered sidewalk. I imagined that I could read the word *disqualified* in the swirls.

Tammy had come out with Mr. Wilson's broom and dustpan in time to hear Dr. Hutch's speech. "Does this mean you lost the contest?" There were tears in her eyes.

"Maybe," I answered. "Probably."

"We could try bleaching the paint out of the sidewalk. My mother uses bleach everywhere in our house," Lisa suggested.

"What's the use? It's over for us." Winning was hopeless now.

"Well, I'm not giving up! We worked too hard on this. Besides, we owe it to Mr. Wilson to leave his sidewalk clean. I'm going to the supermarket to buy a bottle." Lisa could be awfully determined sometimes.

The bleach worked pretty well, although there were still a few stubborn spots of red and black left. "Just one good rainstorm, and you'll never know," Mr. Wilson assured us, after he had inspected the cleanup.

We finished just in time. The judges were already in front of the bakery, examining Stacey and Rachel's window. Leading the group was Mayor Donelli, who is a contest judge every year. Mrs. Coco, the chairwoman of our school's Parents Association, trotted along beside him. Mayor Donelli and Mrs. Coco were followed by two other judges, but Dr. Hutch wasn't with them. Her little car with its flat-as-a-pancake tire was still parked at the curb.

"You must be Amanda and Lisa," Mrs. Coco said, consulting her clipboard.

The little group stared at our window and made some notes on their work sheets. Mayor Donelli looked down at the sidewalk. He whispered something in Mrs. Coco's ear. She frowned and wrote something down. Then the mayor looked at the Volkswagen's flat tire. He made some more notes.

"All right, girls, we're finished," Mrs. Coco finally said. Mayor Donelli patted Tammy on the head, and the group moved on to Sarah and Lacey's window.

"They were smiling! I think they liked it!" Lisa burst out after they'd left.

"Forget it, Lisa. Dr. Hutch will make sure we don't win."

"I want to stay for the awards, anyway," she insisted. "Let's walk around and see the other windows. Then we can go over to the post office. That's where they're announcing the winners."

We walked down Main Street to see the competition.

We agreed that Stacey and Rachel's Christmas tree painting was boring, because it was only made of chocolate chip cookies and chocolate-frosted cupcakes. It needed more color. Then we moved on to the bank window, which had been painted by two sixth graders. It showed a computer printing out a Happy Holidays sign. "So-so," Lisa commented. A little further on at the supermarket, an enormous snowman dripped down the window. It had been painted by a fifth grader we knew in another class.

At the corner, a turkey wearing a Santa suit smiled out from the window of Quick-Dry Cleaners. "This one's pretty good," I admitted.

"Even though a boy did it," Tammy added. It was signed "Don Campbell, Grade Six."

"I don't think I want to see any more windows," Lisa groaned. "It makes me too nervous. Let's go to the post office."

A crowd had already gathered in front of the little brick building. At the foot of the steps, Mayor Donelli, Mrs. Coco, and the other judges joked and laughed together. Dr. Hutch was still nowhere in sight. Finally, Mayor

Donelli straightened his pilgrim hat and walked up the stairs to the landing in front of the doors, where a microphone had been set up.

"Welcome to Hartman's Thirteenth Annual Holiday Window-Painting Contest," he began. "As you know, our little elves have been very busy this morning. I wish they all could win, but this *is* a competition. The judges had to pick the three entries that they thought best displayed originality, artistic quality, and neatness. There were so many good ones, that making our final choices was very difficult. Now, Mrs. Coco, our chairperson, will announce the winners. Before she comes up here, just let me say I hope all you little elves will try again next year."

The part about the little elves was so insulting! But the crowd clapped, and then Mrs. Coco came up to the microphone. Tammy hopped on one foot as she waited for the news.

Mrs. Coco cleared her throat and smiled. "This year's first prize goes to the team of Lacey Lawrence and Sarah Devlin for their painting, *Ice Skating Chipmunks,* on the window of Live Well Pharmacy. Congratulations, girls!"

Lacey and Sarah were somewhere up front. I could hear their squeals above the applause of the crowd, but I couldn't see them.

My throat felt tight and my eyes were burning. I wanted to leave, but I wanted to stay, too. Lisa squeezed my hand. Tammy stopped hopping.

Mrs. Coco held up her hands for quiet. "The second prize goes to Donald Campbell for his *Turkey Santa* on the window of Quick-Dry Cleaners. Congratulations, Donald."

"We still have one more," Mrs. Coco announced, when the crowd was quiet again. "The third prize goes to Amanda Simon and Lisa Krauss for their *Peace on Earth* painting at Wilson's World of Toys. That was a nice sentiment, girls."

I stood there stupidly, not believing what I'd heard, until Tammy threw her arms around me. "You did it! You won a prize!" she shouted. Lisa joined our embrace.

"Winners, come inside and pick up your awards," Mrs. Coco called out.

We joined Lacey, Sarah, and Donald at a long wooden counter. "First prize first," Mrs. Coco said, as she handed Lacey and Sarah each a thin, square package wrapped in holiday paper, plus a single envelope. They ripped the paper off their packages. "The new Wishman Rocker album!" Sarah exclaimed.

Then Lacey opened the envelope. "Wishman tickets!" she announced, waving them in the air. "And there's something else here, too." She unfolded a sheet of paper. "A gift certificate for dinner for two at Poppa's Pizza!"

"Now the second prize," Mrs. Coco said, handing Donald an envelope. He tore it open. Inside was another certificate for dinner at Poppa's—and two tickets to Wishman's concert.

"All right!" he exclaimed.

I held my breath and waited. There was one envelope left. It couldn't be a record album. Were Lisa and I going to get a pizza dinner— or concert tickets?

Mrs. Coco placed the envelope down in front of us.

"You open it, I can't!" I said to Lisa.

"Neither can I!" she answered.

"Want me to do it?" Tammy offered. She took the envelope and tore it open. "Look, it's tickets!" She held them under my nose. "You won tickets!"

We all jumped up and down and hugged

each other. As we stood there scrunched up happily together, the door to the post office opened. In came Dr. Hutch. "I'm glad you're still here," she said. "I want to have a little talk with you."

We untangled ourselves and stood stiffly, like statues. My heart and my head were pounding, and there was a pit in my stomach as deep as the Grand Canyon. We were going to be disqualified after all!

Dr. Hutch looked down at us. She seemed even taller than usual. "After I stopped at the garage, I came back to check the sidewalk in front of Wilson's World of Toys. I saw that you did a very thorough job of cleaning up, and I realized that the broken jar was just an unfortunate accident. I certainly didn't want to penalize you girls unfairly. And your painting was lovely. So I didn't mention my tire to the other judges." Her face crinkled into a smile. "I just wanted to congratulate you!" She took hold of my sweaty, paint-stained hand and shook it.

Soon after Dr. Hutch left, my father pulled up in front of the post office. "How did you do?" he asked, as we piled into the car.

"We won tickets to Wishman's concert!" I burst out.

"That's terrific! Things seem to have worked out exactly as you'd planned." He sounded impressed.

"Not exactly, Dad," I answered. Then Lisa, Tammy, and I told him all about Jonathan, the broken paint jar, and Dr. Hutch's car.

"Do you think the accident kept you from winning first place?" he wanted to know.

I looked at Lisa and she looked at me. "No," we said in unison.

"The other two windows really were better," Lisa said.

The funny thing was, they were—and I didn't even mind.

Tammy's Birthday Surprise

That night I discovered Mom had scheduled Tammy's birthday party for the same day as the concert. I called Lisa right away to see if her mother could take us.

"My mother?" Her voice was high-pitched. "Never! She'd probably have a nervous breakdown from all the noise. My dad would take us if he were here, though."

"I'll see if my dad can take us, and I'll call you back later," I said.

"Well, okay." Lisa sounded reluctant. I think being around my father made her miss hers even more.

Dad came into the kitchen. "Could you take Lisa and me to the concert?" I asked. "It's on

Tammy's birthday, and no one else can do it."

"Gee, thanks." He thought a minute. "What time is the concert?"

"It's at four."

"I think it'll be okay. Tammy's party is from one to four. We'd just have to leave an hour early. Why don't you explain it to her?"

I found Tammy watching a rerun of "Diff'-rent Strokes" that she'd probably seen at least ten times before. "Tammy, I need Daddy to take Lisa and me to the Wishman concert."

"*Shhh.* Arnold's been kidnapped!" she protested.

"You already know he'll get away. This is important."

She sighed dramatically and looked up at me.

"Wishman's concert is the same day as your birthday party."

Her mouth flew open. "You mean you and Daddy are going to miss my party? And the magic show?"

Tammy was having a magician at her party. The magician was actually our neighbors' son, Peter, who would be home from college on his winter break that week.

"We'd just be missing an hour—*after* Peter's

performance. Please, Tammy, you know how hard I worked to get to this concert! You even helped me," I reminded her. "I was hoping Lisa's mom could take us, but she said it would make her too nervous. Dad said he'd go."

"Okay, okay!" Tammy had already turned her attention back to the TV set. "Now could you please be quiet!"

With a sigh of relief, I ran to call Lisa back.

It turned out, though, that I didn't have to worry about missing Tammy's party at all. Because the first present Tammy got on her birthday was the chicken pox. It wasn't even on her list.

Suddenly, the whole house was in an uproar. Mom was busy calling the doctor and the mothers of the kids who had been invited to the party. Dad ran out for a box of oatmeal to put in Tammy's bath water, because it's supposed to be soothing for itchy skin. From her room, Tammy hollered that she was thirsty. I poured some orange juice and brought it up to her.

"I hate orange," Tammy scowled as I handed it to her.

"You liked it yesterday."

"Can't I have what I like?" she whined. "I want apple."

I thumped downstairs for the apple juice and took it back up. It wasn't fair! Tammy was the one with chicken pox. Why did I have to suffer, too?

I decided to phone Lisa. "Tammy has the chicken pox, and Mom and Dad are acting like she's dying," I complained.

"On her birthday! That's too bad," Lisa said.

I could feel a hot flush spread over my face. Tammy didn't need Lisa's sympathy; she already had enough people worrying about her. I wanted her to feel sorry for me! "We've still got hours before the concert, and I've got nothing to do. We didn't even get to have the chocolate chip pancakes Mom always makes on family birthdays," I sulked.

"Did you write up your wish?" Lisa asked. "I'm working on mine now."

"Not yet! With all the fuss over the chicken pox, I almost forgot."

"I read in a magazine that Wishman gave this girl and her whole family tickets to see a concert he was doing in Australia. He flew them all over there in his private plane," Lisa gushed. "And at another show, he let a boy use his limousine and chauffeur for a day!"

I imagined myself arriving at school in a shiny, silver limo. It was kind of exciting, but I wasn't going to waste a wish on it. "What are you asking for?"

"I want a plane ticket to Japan so I can visit my father this summer. He'll probably never be able to afford a ticket for me; he's always short of money. My mother says he never learned how to save a nickel."

"Then I hope Wishman chooses yours," I said, really meaning it.

"Maybe he'll pick both of ours! What are you going to ask for?"

"I don't know. I'll think of something now," I said. "We'll come by for you at three!"

What could I wish for? All the things I came up with—a typewriter, a white Persian cat, a 35-millimeter camera—seemed selfish and unimportant compared with Lisa's request.

While I sat at the kitchen table thinking, Mom came in and phoned Presto Peter to cancel his performance. "Maybe we could reschedule for next weekend," I heard her say. "Oh, you're going back to school on Monday? You won't be coming home again until Christmas vacation? That's too bad. Perhaps next year, then."

Suddenly I felt sorry for Tammy. I knew how much she had been looking forward to her party and Peter's performance. Then I got a brainstorm: Why not wish for Wishman to come to our house and give Tammy her own private concert after the show tonight!

I ran up to my room and took out my stationery with the lavender paper and the pen that writes in purple, grape-scented ink. In my neatest handwriting, I wrote my wish. It was worth a try.

Wishman

Lisa came running out of her house as soon as we pulled up. She had on this incredible denim jacket with a pink satin collar and cuffs, and the whole thing was faded to make it look old.

"Where did you get that jacket!" I gasped, as she opened the car door.

"My dad sent it to me as a good-bye present. Look at the back!" She whirled around so I could see a heart made of rhinestones in the center.

"It's really, really beautiful!"

"I know! I love it! My mother thinks it's too expensive for a kid."

The front of the marquee outside the Hartman Music Hall said Welcome Home for the

Holidays, Wishman! On each side of the marquee, there was another message: All 675 Seats in This Theatre Have Been Sold Out! Up and down the street, vendors were selling tee shirts with Wishman's picture on them, little flags that said Wishman Put the Heart in Hartman, and buttons that said Ronald Flugelman, We Knew You When, with a picture of Wishman as a little boy wearing a cowboy hat. While we waited, my dad bought Lisa and me each a button.

Finally, the line started moving. As we went through the doors, we heard the ticket takers shouting, "If you've brought a wish, drop it in one of the collection baskets at the head of each aisle. I patted my pocket; my wish was still there. Lisa held hers, rolling a corner back and forth nervously.

"Row Q, use the door to the left," the ticket taker told my dad, handing him back the stubs.

"Follow me." Dad pushed through the crowd. I clung tightly to his belt and Lisa held my hand so we wouldn't get separated. At the head of our aisle, there was a plain, gray wire garbage can filled with wishes. We smiled and dropped ours in. Dad waved us on to Row Q. Lacey, Sarah, and Sarah's mother were already there. A little further down the row, I saw Donald with an older boy who was probably his brother.

"Hi! Did you bring a wish?" Lacey asked us.

"Uh-huh. I asked for a trip to Japan," Lisa answered, without explaining why.

"I wished for a private concert," I added, without saying for whom.

Dad raised his eyebrows and rolled his eyes when he heard this. "At home? I hope you cleaned your room this morning, Mandy."

"All I want is a pair of white fringed boots, a studded leather jacket, and a food processor," Lacey announced.

"A food processor?" Dad asked.

"For my mother. Her birthday is next week."

On the stage, a work crew was setting up drums and keyboards and testing microphones. The lights flashed on and off for a moment, and the audience got a little quieter. Mayor Donelli walked up on the stage. He was wearing a Santa hat.

"What's he doing here?" Lacey asked.

Lisa covered her eyes with her hand. "I hope he's not going to make another speech."

"Howdy, Hartmanites!" the mayor said into the microphone. A terrible electric hum pierced our ears. Someone ran across the stage to adjust the sound system. "This is a proud moment for Hartman, as one of our most distinguished citizens returns to pay his respects to his hometown," the mayor continued.

The crowd was restless. "Go barf in your hat, Donelli!" someone shouted from the audience.

"I know you're anxious for the concert to begin, but please, let's remember our manners," the mayor said. He had to yell over the din of the audience. "As I was saying, Hartman is proud of Wishman, or Ronald Flugelman as his friends and neighbors still know him. And judging by his return home, I'd say that Ronald is proud of Hartman. I'm just here to say thank you, Ronald. You kids out in the audience should follow the example that Ronald has set. Follow your dreams, and someday you too may be stars. Bless you all!"

"He must be up for reelection," Dad groaned.

The lights dimmed and Wishman's band took their places on the stage. The audience went bananas. I recognized a few of the musicians from the rock videos I'd seen on TV, especially Slide, Wishman's drummer. He had a long, droopy mustache and eyes that always looked like they were crying. Actually, I was too far back to see his eyes. As the band tuned their electric guitars and keyboards, a few twangs drifted out toward us.

And then, without any introduction, Wishman bounded out from the wings, with his frizzy, shoulder-length hair flying behind him and the studs on his black leather jacket twinkling in the glow of the stage lights. The audience screamed. I could feel my whole body shaking with excitement. Someone was shrieking in my ear. Suddenly I realized it was me! I'd caught Wishman fever! The band went straight into the opening number, a song called "Give Me Toe Jam," and the crowd quieted down.

> *Soft and fuzzy little balls*
> *Hiding there wedged in the walls*
> *Between your little toesies tight*
> *Waiting for you every night—*
> *Toe jam!*

When the song was over, Wishman finally spoke. "Like the mayor said, I'm glad to be back. It was great growin' up here, except when I had to go to school. Ha, ha! That's a joke, you guys. Anyway, because this is my hometown, I'll be pickin' three wishes to grant at the end of the concert. Good luck, you guys."

He wasn't much of a speaker, but I clapped and stomped my feet along with everyone else.

Wishman sang eleven songs. He also danced and strutted and sweated and moaned and yelled and strummed his guitar and drummed his guitar and lay down on the stage and rolled around on the stage and leaped off the stage and kissed someone in the first row and hopped back on the stage and told a few jokes and ripped off his shirt and threw it into the audience and drank a can of Pepsi and tied a sweatband around his head and climbed up on a stool and jumped down off the stool onto his guitar (and smashed it) and finally collapsed in a heap. Slide revived him by dousing him with a glass of water.

It was an exciting show, but it was also kind of weird. Some parts, like when Wishman rolled around and told jokes, were funny; others, like when he smashed his guitar and collapsed, were sort of scary. Maybe if I won the wish contest, our house would be destroyed by the time Tammy's private concert was over.

Then Slide played a drumroll, and Wishman shouted, "It's time for the moment you guys have been waiting for—wish time!"

He ran offstage and came back pushing a large, purple box on wheels with a panel of dials on top and a circular door on its front. It looked like a clothes dryer painted purple; in fact, it was a clothes dryer!

"Your wishes were all dumped in the wish box earlier. To be absolutely fair, we turned this thing on backstage and mixed 'em all up," he explained. He opened the dryer, stuck his hand in, and pulled out the first wish. I was too far back to see whether the paper was purple.

"Louise Burns," Wishman read. There was a shriek from the audience. "You've asked for a super-deluxe-jumbo-gigantic-sized-incredibly-loud-tape-deck-box-radio. Congratulations, we are gonna get you one so big, so loud, and so jumbo deluxe, you'll get a hernia from carrying it home!"

"Yes! Yes! Yes!" I could hear Louise screeching.

"Hang in there, Louise, old girl," Wishman said. "We've still got two more wishes to go." He put his hand back into the dryer and pulled out another crumpled paper. I held my breath.

"Here's a guy who wants my guitar—David Schwartz!" Wishman announced. He walked over to where his smashed guitar lay on the stage and picked it up. "Dave, I hope you didn't want one you could play." There were hoots from the audience. "Only kidding, Dave. I've got lots more of these," Wishman said. "The crew will make sure you get one with strings."

Now the entire audience quieted down. It was everyone's last chance. Lisa squeezed my arm.

Wishman plucked out a wish and opened it slowly. "Mindy Simon! Where are you Mindy?"

My stomach did a double flip. Did he mean Mandy Simon?

"Maybe it's you!" Lisa squeaked.

"Mindy, are you out there?" Wishman asked again. "Don't be shy."

"I think he means you, *Mindy,*" Dad wise-cracked. "You'd better stand up."

I was frozen in my seat. I couldn't move. Together, Lisa and Dad shoved me up and helped me climb on the chair.

"Hey, a midget fan!" Wishman said. A spotlight suddenly shone on my face. It was so bright I couldn't see. Maybe I'd be deaf and blind by the time this concert was over!

"Let's see. You've asked me to sing a song

for your sister, Tammy, who has the chicken pox," Wishman said. "That's real nice of you. I'll dedicate this next one to her. Let's hear it for Tammy."

The audience whistled and cheered.

Couldn't Wishman read? That wasn't what I'd wished! I wanted him to come home with me and sing to Tammy tonight! In person! My note said "a private concert."

"But I want you to come home with me and sing to Tammy," my voice quavered. It was no use. He couldn't hear me over all the noise. I guess he didn't want to hear me.

I stood there stupidly with the spotlight on me while Wishman sang his hit song, "My Heart's Like a Doughnut Without You."

Bake shop girl, look what you've done.
Since you're gone I'm like a bun.
Worse than a pumpernickel roll,
My poor heart, it's got a hole.
Now I hope you're havin' fun!

At the end of the concert, Wishman told the winners to stop at the box office for a special surprise. Dad, Lisa, and I had to push our way through the exiting crowds to get there.

"Mindy Simon?" a man asked, as I peered through the plastic ticket window.

"It's *Mandy,*" I told him.

"I have something for you from Wishman," he said, thrusting a big manila envelope into my hands.

I was feeling pretty angry with Wishman for cheating me out of my real wish. But maybe there were tickets inside for another concert for Tammy and me or an invitation to meet him another time.

I waited until we got into the car to open it. It was only a large, glossy, black-and-white picture of Wishman. Across the top he'd scrawled a message: *To Mindy, whose wish I have granted today—Wishman.*

Cheering Up
Tammy

At home, I went right up to see Tammy. Her presents had been unwrapped and were scattered all over the floor of her room. She was lying in bed with our cat, Harry, who's as loyal as any dog could ever be. I wondered whether cats could get chicken pox.

"Gee, these are great, Tam," I said, looking at the gymnast doll she'd fallen in love with at Wilson's toy store and the glow-in-the-dark markers I'd given her. "Can this doll really do a flip?"

"I didn't try it yet," she answered. Her face was blotchy, and one of her eyelids was swollen where she had a chicken pox blister.

"C'mon, Tammy, cheer up! This chicken pox

will be over in a few days," I said. "Do you want to play your new Chinese checkers game with me?"

"Not now. I'm too tired."

"How about if I read you some of these riddles?" I offered, holding up a new riddle book.

"Uh-uh. Not now."

"Well, maybe I'll just read them to Harry," I said, sitting down on the bed and flipping to the first page. "What did the Easter bunny say to the pediatrician?"

Before Tammy or Harry could answer, the door bell rang. "I'll get it!" I called. Tammy was so grumpy, I was glad for an excuse to get away.

Who could be at the door, anyway? It was 7:30 on a Saturday night and my sister had chicken pox. Oh my God! Maybe Wishman had come to sing to Tammy after all! Maybe he'd reread my wish after the concert and realized that I'd asked him to come sing to Tammy in person. He probably felt sort of dumb for misreading it in the first place, for thinking he'd granted my wish when he really hadn't. Was my hair combed? Was my room a mess? Well, it didn't matter—he'd be singing in Tammy's room, anyway.

Could this really be happening?

The bell rang again, just as I got downstairs. I looked through the little window in the door. His face was turned away, but sure enough, there was the famous frizzy hair and studded leather jacket. Next to him was a big black trunk. His guitar was probably in there. My heart was pounding wildly.

"Mandy, who is it, honey?" Mom asked, coming out of the kitchen. "Open the door."

My fingers shook as I turned the lock and pulled the door open. Wishman turned to me with a smile.

Only it wasn't Wishman. It was Presto Peter, our neighbor-magician.

"Hi Amanda Panda," he said, patting me on the head like I was still a little kid.

"What are you doing here?" I grumbled.

"My date for tonight came down with the flu, and since I was free, I called your mom and offered to give Tammy a private performance. You certainly don't look very happy to see me."

"Come on in, Peter," Mom called out from behind me. "I think we could all use a little cheering up."

"I brought the whole show along," Peter

said, waving at the trunk. "The works." I helped him wheel it in. It sure was heavy.

"So, Mandy, your mom told me you went to see the Wishman concert today. How was it?" Peter asked, as we lugged the trunk upstairs.

I had to think about it. I still wasn't sure how I felt.

"Actually, it was a lot like a magic show," I finally said. "The music, the lights, and the crowd screaming made Wishman seem as though he was something more than a person." We stopped and rested the trunk on the steps for a minute. "Wishman granted wishes like he was the Wizard of Oz, but he was really just a humbug like the wizard, too. He pretended to make mine come true, but he didn't. And no one in the crowd even knew that he was faking, except me."

Peter was staring at me in amazement. "You mean Wishman actually picked your wish!"

"Yeah, but you know what's even more incredible?" I suddenly felt myself grinning.

"What?"

"You're the one who's going to make it come true!"

Red Junior

"I left some nice, hot oatmeal on the table for you," Mom said, when I came down for breakfast Monday morning. "I'll just take this tray up to Tammy." On the tray was a glass of orange juice, a glass of milk, and a bowl of oatmeal. On top of the oatmeal, Mom had made a smiley face out of raisins, with a few extra plastered on the cheeks and forehead.

I wondered how Tammy could still eat oatmeal after having to bathe in it. As soon as Mom was gone, I scraped out my own bowl into the cat's dish. "Here, Harry, have some breakfast," I coaxed.

Good old Harry jumped down off the windowsill and padded over. Harry will eat almost anything.

I opened the pantry closet, found the Oreos, and stuffed one in my mouth and three in my jacket pocket. I also found a Colonel Crunch granola bar and shoved that in my shirt pocket, in case I needed a snack later. Then I picked up my books and my lunch bag. "Bye Mom, bye Tammy," I yelled up the stairs.

"Have a good day," Mom called back.

As soon as I got to class, I knew something was up. There was a lot of excited whispering going on, and Jonathan was standing up front next to Mr. Popper's desk. He looked very upset.

Finally Mr. P. signaled for us to quiet down. "You've all met Jonathan's rooster, R.J.," he began. "When Jonathan went out to his back-yard to feed R.J. this morning, the cage door was unlatched and R.J. was gone."

"Hey, Jonathan, maybe your mother is making fried chicken tonight," Danny called out.

"Maybe your mother is making fried dog meat," Jonathan shot back.

"That's enough, boys," Mr. Popper said. "As you know, farm roosters like my own Red are pretty tough birds, but around here, life can be dangerous for them. Remember that first-grade joke, 'Why did the chicken cross the road?' Well, if a chicken really tried to cross the road, it could easily be run over. And although a farmer's dogs and cats are trained to leave the chickens alone, most pets don't know any better. So we need to help find R.J. before something happens to him." He turned to Jonathan. "Tell us what we can do to help you."

"After school, I'm going to put up LOST posters around the neighborhood. Does anyone want to help me?" Jonathan asked.

Paul and Matthew raised their hands.

"And if anyone sees R.J., grab him and call me. I'll come get him right away. Whatever you do, don't let him out of your sight."

"Better write your telephone number on the board," Mr. P. told Jonathan. "Everyone copy it down and keep a lookout for R.J. after school. Are there any questions?"

"How do you pick up a rooster?" Stacey wanted to know.

"From underneath. You rest his chest against the palm of your hand," Jonathan explained.

"Anyone else?" Mr. P. asked.

Sarah raised her hand. "Does he bite?"

"Aw, he just pecks a little. He can't really hurt you."

Baloney! I thought, remembering when Mr. P.'s Red had attacked me at the farm.

Anyway, my plans for the afternoon certainly did not include looking for a rooster. Lisa had convinced me to meet her at the park to shoot some hoops. She wants to be on the girls' team when we get to junior high. I'm not too hot at basketball, even though my dad's always trying to get me to play with him.

I stopped home to drop off my books before meeting Lisa. "Hi! I'm in here," Mom called out, when she heard me come in the front door. I followed her voice to the family room. There she was on her knees, folding clothes into a basket. I recognized an old quilted jumper and a fuzzy red sweater that were too small for Tammy to wear anymore. There was tons more stuff, too.

"How was school?"

"Okay. Where's Tammy?"

"Upstairs napping." She folded the last item, a red windbreaker, and dropped it on top of the pile. "I'd like you to take these old clothes over to Mrs. Becker for Cindy and Debbie," she said.

"Now? I'm supposed to meet Lisa at the park," I protested.

"This won't take very long. You can put this basket in the wagon and wheel it over there. Besides, the Beckers' house is on the way to the park."

Actually, I didn't mind going over to the Beckers'. Cindy and Debbie were really cute kids, and they always made a big fuss over me. I figured it wouldn't take very long to drop off the clothes and say hi. I could even leave the wagon there and pick it up on my way home.

I dragged the basket outside and plopped it into the old red wagon. I remembered when Dad used to pull Tammy and me into town. Sometimes, Tammy tried to give Harry a ride, but he wouldn't stay put. Now we mostly used the wagon for doing errands.

The Beckers lived just beyond our school. I could even take a shortcut right across the school yard to get there. I walked as fast as I could. On every corner there was a sign posted on a tree or a telephone pole that said:

MISSING—A ROOSTER
ANSWERS TO THE NAME RED JUNIOR OR R.J.
IF FOUND, PLEASE CALL ME RIGHT AWAY.

JONATHAN ADLER, 555–0793

Jonathan was working fast. He actually lived on the other side of school, on the same block as the Beckers, but he'd already gotten his posters over to my street.

I remembered how terrible I'd felt when Harry was lost. He was just a kitten, and we'd let him out to play in the backyard. But when I called him in, he was missing. We looked all over the neighborhood. We even called the police. Finally, that night after I was in bed, our doorbell rang. It was Mrs. Foley from across the street, with Harry in her arms. She'd found him in her basement. He must have crawled through an open window to get away from a dog or something.

By the time I got to the school, I was actually feeling sorry for Jonathan. I pulled the wagon across the empty yard toward the Beckers'. Suddenly I heard a loud commotion over in the corner by the tall chain-link fence. Three dogs had gathered together, barking excitedly. I headed toward them to see what was going on. Once I'd watched a group of dogs that had cornered a big bullfrog. They had made a lot of noise, but they were afraid to get too close to the strange, green hopping thing.

When I got a closer look, my bones jumped inside my skin! Backed up against the fence was Red Junior! He was flapping and squawking and nipping the air, but he didn't look like any match for those dogs!

The dogs yelped and snarled at R.J. The scariest one, a big, black Doberman, seemed to be the leader of the pack. It drooled hungrily, and when it barked, the other two—a shaggy mutt and a hound—joined in. In response, R.J. lifted a sharp-clawed foot and struck the air in front of the Doberman's nose. The dog gave a low growl and bared his spiky teeth.

I looked around for help, but the school yard was empty. Then I noticed a branch nearly as thick as a baseball bat lying on the ground. I bent down slowly, trying not to attract the dogs' attention. As I stood up, the Doberman began barking. R.J. screeched a hoarse response.

"Stop! Go away!" I screamed at the dogs. My voice sounded squeaky, and I was shaking all over.

The dogs ignored me. They were prancing around R.J., closing in. "No! *No!*" I shouted. I thwacked the branch against the ground. That got their attention. They quieted down and looked me over. Only R.J. kept up his nervous mutterings.

"Shoo! Go home!" I commanded, trying to

make my voice sound firm. I shook the branch at them.

In an instant, the hound opened its mouth and leaped at my outstretched arm. I screamed as I waited for the sharp feel of its teeth in my flesh. Instead, it grasped the branch and yanked it loose from my grip. Then it wagged its tail and trotted off with its prize.

The shaggy mutt glanced over at R.J., then back at the hound. I held my breath and prayed. Finally, it took off after the hound in a playful chase.

For a minute, I was overjoyed—until the Doberman began its low, threatening growls again. I looked back at R.J. The poor thing just sat glassy-eyed in the corner, its feathers all puffed out like a sick bird's. The Doberman advanced.

"Get away! Get away!" I yelled. But when the dog turned its mean-eyed face toward me, my knees shook like they were on springs. That beast was terrifying!

My heart was beating very fast. I put my hand over it to try to calm down and think what to do, when I felt something in my shirt pocket. The Colonel Crunch granola bar!

I unwrapped it quickly. "Here doggie," I called. The dog had its jaws open; its saliva was dripping onto R.J.'s ruffled feathers. "Look doggie, candy!" I said, waving the bar in the air, hoping it would catch the scent.

Would a dog choose Colonel Crunch over a chicken dinner? If so, what a great candy commercial this could make!

"Come on, you big pig! Come get it!" I urged, desperately. With the Doberman watching, I tossed the granola bar a few feet behind me. If the dog went for it, I knew I'd have to act fast.

The Doberman took a last look at R.J. and skulked off reluctantly to get my snack. As soon as it moved, I dumped out the clothes in the laundry basket. Then I scooped up Red Junior, put him in the wagon, and clapped the basket over him so that he couldn't get out— and the dog couldn't get in.

I left the monster savoring the last of the Colonel Crunch bar and pulled R.J. out of the school yard.

On the way to Jonathan's, I wondered what he would say when he saw R.J. After all the trouble he'd caused me, he certainly didn't deserve what I'd done for him. He probably wouldn't even appreciate how I'd risked my life for his dumb rooster. Well, who cared? At least I was proud of myself.

As I wheeled the wagon down the block, I could see Jonathan outside on the driveway, shooting a basketball at a hoop over the garage door. He wasn't making a single basket. He didn't seem to be trying.

"What are you doing here?" Jonathan asked grumpily, as I turned in at his house.

I couldn't help smiling. "Actually, I have something for you. Look under the basket."

Jonathan eyed me skeptically. Then he lifted up the basket. "R.J.!"

The bird's eyes seemed to brighten a little.

"What happened? Where did you find him?"

While I told him about the dogs in the school yard, Jonathan cuddled the bird. For once he listened without wisecracking.

"Gee. Thanks a million for saving him," he said. "You're pretty brave."

Coming from Jonathan, that was a real compliment. I felt a happy little glow, and I knew my cheeks were turning pink. It was the only nice thing Jonathan had ever said to me, and it felt kind of good.

"Well, I've got to get going now. I have to go

back to the school yard and pick up the clothes for the Beckers—unless that Doberman has eaten them, too." I put the empty basket in the wagon and turned to leave.

"Mandy, wait!" Jonathan said suddenly. "I'll help you. Just let me put R.J. back in his cage."

"Don't forget to put the latch on this time," I reminded him. "I'm out of Colonel Crunch bars!"

A Message
from the Spirits

Lisa and I had a date to spend the next Saturday together. On my way to her house, I decided to check up on R.J. Lisa lives on the same side of the school yard as Jonathan and the Beckers, so it wasn't really out of my way.

Jonathan was in the driveway shooting baskets again, only this time he was making most of them. R.J. was strutting around on the porch. When I approached, he flapped his wings and hopped down the steps, crowing threateningly.

"Hold on, R.J.! Mandy's your friend," Jonathan said, grabbing him. The rooster clucked grumblingly, irritated at having his plan of attack spoiled. Jonathan smiled at me. "Want to shoot some baskets?"

137

"I just stopped by to see how your old rooster was doing," I explained. "I'm on my way to Lisa's."

"He's back to his mean old self." Jonathan stroked Red Junior's back as he spoke.

"I can see that!" Suddenly, I didn't know what else to say. For the first time, I noticed what nice blue eyes Jonathan had; bright like a summer sky.

"Maybe we could have a game some other time." Jonathan nodded at the hoop.

"Oh. Sure," I agreed. "Once in a while, I play with Lisa or my Dad on the driveway, but I'm not too good at it." Actually I'd only played basketball twice with my father all year, and he'd practically had to beg me. But the idea of playing with Jonathan seemed more interesting.

"I could teach you," he offered. "Anyway, the more you play, the better you get."

"Okay. But I have to get going now. Lisa's expecting me."

Jonathan picked up the basketball and tossed it casually toward the hoop. It slipped right through. "See you in school."

I practiced dribbling an imaginary basketball the rest of the way to Lisa's. She opened the door before I could even knock. "Hi!" she said, excitedly. "Come on upstairs. I've got something to show you." As usual, her room was neat. The only thing out of place was a newspaper, strewn all around on her bed. "Look at this!" She pointed to a page.

I looked down at the paper. "You're excited because Foodland is having a sale on lamb chops?"

"Not that! Look at this ad for the contest Molson's Travel Agency is having."

I read the ad. "Let Molson's Travel Send You to Japan," the headline said. Then it described how terrific a trip to Japan could be, from a traditional tea ceremony to their new Disneyland. It sure sounded good to me; I'd never even been to Disneyland in America. To win, all you had to do was send them an essay describing your most memorable trip ever. The person who wrote the best essay would get an all-expense-paid vacation to Japan for two.

"I've entered enough contests this year to last me the rest of my life. No thanks," I said. I meant it, too. The window-painting contest and Wishman's contest had been enough for me. There were just too many chances to be upset or disappointed. And I didn't like competing against my friends, either.

"Not you, *me!*" Lisa burst out, impatiently.

"*I'm* going to enter this one so I can win those plane tickets. That way I can visit my father!"

"Oh, right!" I slapped my forehead, feeling stupid for not realizing.

"If I don't win, I just know he won't be able to afford the airfare to fly me out there." She twisted a strand of her hair. "Mom's always reminding me how irresponsible he is about money."

"You're going to win this contest!" I assured her. "You always get A's in writing. Besides, I just feel like you'll win, and I'm usually right about these things." Actually I'm not a good guesser at all, but I would've said anything to make her feel better.

"You really think so?" Lisa brightened. She wanted to believe me as much as I wanted her to. Suddenly she jumped up off the bed. "Let's ask the Ouija board for an answer!"

Lisa is the only person I know who has a *real* Ouija board, the old-fashioned, wooden kind painted with mysterious shapes and symbols. Even her spirit indicator is made of polished wood with a crystal window in it. It actually belongs to her mother. Mrs. Krauss once told us that when she was a girl, she was always checking with the spirits about important things. I have a Ouija board from the toy store that someone once gave me for a birthday present. It's the kind that's made of plastic with dumb-looking winged people flying across it. The spirit indicator has a fuzzy plastic window, too. You could never contact the spirits with one of those.

Lisa and I had used the Ouija board once before when our fourth-grade teacher, Mrs. Brooks, was pregnant. We wanted to know if she was having a boy or a girl, because we were going to crochet a pair of booties as a going-away present.

The board spelled out *g-i-r-l,* so we each made a pink bootie. But a few weeks after "it" was born, we got a thank-you note from "baby William." Lisa said the board hadn't worked because I had talked too much while we were using it. You had to take the spirits seriously.

"Close the door," Lisa ordered, as she unpacked the board from its box. She pulled down the shades and drew the curtains. It was pretty dark.

"Do you have to do that?" I asked.

"You know spirits don't like light!"

We sat side by side on her bed with our legs hanging down and laid the board across our laps. Then we placed our fingers lightly on the spirit indicator and closed our eyes.

"Spirits from the other world, please fill this room," Lisa droned.

I felt a shiver run down my spine. One spirit would have been enough for me. Why did we have to ask for a whole roomful?

"What are we waiting for?" I whispered.

"For all the spirits to get here. Now be quiet!"

After a minute, Lisa spoke in her "spirit voice" again. "Welcome all friendly spirits. Thank you for coming." Then she nudged me with her elbow. "Thank them, Mandy," she whispered, impatiently. "They have to feel wanted."

I hoped she was right about them being friendly. "I'm, um, glad you're here," I said, feeling stupid and nervous at the same time.

"Spirits, please tell me. Will I win a trip to visit my father in Japan?" Lisa whispered.

Underneath my fingertips, the spirit indicator had been perfectly still. But now I felt it beginning to move ever so slightly. I tried to tell myself that I was imagining it, but my fingers felt the spirit indicator tremble and then creep along the board, directed by some

mysterious force. Then, suddenly, it stopped. I held my breath and shut my eyes even tighter. I was afraid to see what was there.

"I think they've answered," Lisa whispered. "Let's open our eyes on the count of three. One, two, three!"

I kept my eyes closed an extra second. If any spirits were still around, I wanted Lisa to deal with them. Suddenly she let out a blood-curdling shriek.

"What? *What?*" I shouted, covering my face with my hands.

"Mandy, the spirit indicator landed on *yes*! It says YES!"

"Great," I answered weakly, opening my eyes. There didn't seem to be any spirits around. I looked down at the board. The indicator was resting right on the Ouija's *yes* message, underneath a smiling yellow sun. I felt as limp as the old Raggedy Ann doll propped on Lisa's pillow.

I flopped back on the bed, exhausted. "Could you open the curtains now?"

She went over to the window and drew them back. "Mandy? You have to promise that you won't tell anyone I'm entering this contest. Not even your mother."

"Does your mother know?" I asked.

"No! And I'm not going to tell her, either. She's always complaining to me about Dad. I don't want her to know how bad I feel about his going to Japan. I don't want to hurt my mother, but I love him, too! I've got to see him. He needs me. Please, Mandy, you have to keep this a secret," she pleaded.

"Don't worry. I won't tell anyone," I vowed. More than anything in the world, I wanted her to win.

How Not to Win
an Essay Contest

The entry deadline for the contest was only three weeks away. After school on Monday, Lisa rushed home to work on her essay. I did my homework and read some of *Pinballs.* I made my bed and even put away the clean laundry Mom had left on my dresser. Tammy was at her friend Betsey's. There was still an hour until dinner. I decided to call Lisa.

"Hi! How's your essay going?"

"You raisin brain, I haven't even started yet! I'm still deciding between my most memorable vacations," she said, cheerfully.

"Which vacations?"

"Well, I could either tell about that camping trip my dad and I took to Maine when the raccoons stole our food or the trip my mom and I

146

took to Niagara Falls when we met Michael J. Fox's cousin."

"They'd both make good stories," I said.

"I know. And actually, if you weren't on the phone, I'd be starting on one of them right now."

"Okay, okay! I'm getting off in a minute. How about coming over tomorrow? Mom's doing an article on teaching children to cook their favorite foods, and we're going to make our own pizza."

"Don't tempt me! I really have to work on my essay."

"Sorry." I felt guilty for suggesting it. "I'll save you a slice. Good luck! See you tomorrow."

By the middle of the week, Lisa began acting strangely. We were sitting at our usual table in the stuffy, noisy cafeteria. The room smelled of the day's hot lunch—chunky chili—which most of the kids called upchuck chili. Lisa hadn't touched her tuna fish.

"What's wrong?" I asked, as I ate my peanut butter sandwich.

"Nothing. I'm not hungry."

"So, what did you pick for your essay topic?"

"*Shhh!* I told you no one's supposed to know about it."

"No one's even close by." Lacey and Sarah

had already finished their lunches and gone outside. At the far end of our table, Stacey and Danielle were trading baseball cards.

"I just don't want to talk about it now," Lisa said. She sounded angry.

"Okay, I'm sorry. Do you want to sleep over this weekend? I'll ask my mom to rent us a movie."

"I can't go anywhere until I finish my essay. I don't think I'll be finished by then."

"Want me to come over and keep you company? I could do our homework and you could copy it. That way, you'd have more time to write."

"No thanks. I can't concentrate with anyone else around."

For the rest of the week, I tried hard to be understanding about why Lisa didn't have any time for me. But I still couldn't help feeling lonely and a little grumpy each afternoon when I came home from school. Finally, on Saturday, I was desperate. I took Dad's basketball out of the garage and bounced it over to Jonathan's. When I got there, he was out on the driveway with Paul and Matt. Jonathan didn't say a word as I approached, and he definitely did not look glad to see me, so I just kept on bouncing right past his house.

"Hey, Mandy, where are you going with that basketball?" Paul called.

"To Lisa's. We're practicing for the girls' junior high team," I lied.

"You dribble better with your mouth," Matt observed. They all cracked up.

"Come on, guys, let's play." Jonathan picked up his basketball and darted around them, teasingly. In an instant, all three were side-stepping and twisting their way up the driveway toward the hoop.

As soon as I was out of sight, I put the ball under my arm and ran up the rest of the block. At the corner, I realized I couldn't really go to Lisa's. I knew she was busy working on her essay and wouldn't want to be interrupted. To get back home without passing Jonathan's, I had to take a long detour around the neighborhood.

I'd left my home feeling lonely, but when I returned, I was feeling embarrassed, irritated—and pooped. I'd been dumb to think Jonathan would be glad to see me.

A whole week had gone by since Lisa started working on her essay, but on Monday morning she was still acting kind of touchy, and she was still busy after school. A couple of afternoons I played with Tammy, but her favorite games were Headache and Sorry! which are so Boring! We tried checkers, but I won every game and that made her mad. I finished *Pin-balls* and started *Anne of Green Gables* because it had a lot of pages.

By Friday, I'd practically given up on Lisa. I was lying on the sofa in the family room watching TV. I had out the pretzels, chips, popcorn, and cookies. Orange juice, too. My books were scattered on the floor.

I heard the front door open. "I'm home, family!" Dad called. He always comes home early on Fridays.

"I'll be down soon" Mom yelled. "I'm on the phone."

"Mandy, Tammy, where are you two?"

"Tammy's over at Betsey's, but I'm in here, Dad."

Dad bounded into the family room. "How would you like to . . ." Then he slipped on my science book, tripped over my math book, stepped into the popcorn bowl, and spilled chips, pretzels, cookies, and juice everywhere as he fell!

"Are you okay?" I asked. I leaped off the sofa to help him.

"Mandy!" he thundered, "how could you be

so careless? All you've done for the past week is lie on that couch and mope! You don't even put your things away! What is wrong with you, anyway?"

"I'm sorry, Daddy," I said. "Let me help you up." I took his arm and tried to pull him up off the floor.

"Let go. You've done enough around here." He pulled his arm away.

Then Mom came in. She took a look at my damp, crumby father and burst out laughing! "I'm sorry, but you look like someone in a snack-food commercial gone wrong! Are you hurt?"

Dad shook his head.

When she looked at me, she wasn't laughing anymore. "Mandy, it should take you the rest of the afternoon to clean up this disaster area, but at least you'll have something to do! When you're finished, go over to Betsey's and walk Tammy home."

I made sure to do an especially good job of cleaning up the family room. By the time we were all sitting around the dinner table, Dad seemed to have forgotten his accident.

"How's the play coming?" Mom asked Tammy. Her class was putting on *Rumpelstilt-*

skin, and she was going to be the poor miller's daughter who had to spin straw into gold.

Tammy scrunched up her face. "Mrs. Rodriguez had this really dumb idea. She wants us to use spaghetti instead of straw," she complained.

"What's she going to use for gold?" I asked.

Tammy looked heavenward and heaved a big sigh. "Cornflakes! The stage looks like a supermarket," she grumbled. "The whole audience is going to laugh."

Mom looked at me. "Mandy, I've been meaning to ask you why Lisa hasn't been around lately. Did something happen between you two?"

"No, she's just been busy, that's all." Actually, I wished I could say what was really going on. I was beginning to worry about what would happen if Lisa didn't win the contest. But a promise is a promise.

"I almost forgot!" Dad said suddenly. "When I was at the gym this morning, Dan Ferguson gave me his tickets to the Musketeers' game for tomorrow afternoon. He and his family will be away this weekend."

"Gee, I'm sorry," Mom said, "but tomorrow I've got to work on that article I'm doing about family vacations."

I couldn't help groaning as a picture of our family, loaded down with backpacks, trekking across a hot desert, sprang into my mind. Sometimes, Mom came up with some pretty weird ideas.

"Actually, Dan only gave me three tickets," Dad confessed. "I thought I'd take Tammy and Mandy."

"I can't go either. I'm playing at Betsey's tomorrow," Tammy said.

"I'd love to go!" I burst out.

"You would?" Dad sounded amazed.

"Sure!" Anything was better than spending another Saturday alone.

Dad grinned with pleasure. "I'm glad to see you're developing an interest in basketball, Mandy. Since we have an extra ticket, maybe you'd like to bring Lisa along?"

I ran off to the phone. "Lisa, guess what?" I began, when she answered. "My father has three tickets for the Musketeers' game tomorrow afternoon. Do you want to go?"

"Oh Mandy, you know I can't," she answered, dully. "I have to work on my essay. I only have a few more days before the contest ends."

"Come on, Lisa!" I exploded. "Everyone takes a break on the weekend. It's just for a few hours. You need some time off. I think you're taking this essay thing too seriously."

"No, Mandy. You're not taking it seriously enough. Your father is here with you." Her voice was angry.

"Okay, I'll just ask someone else," I told her. But as soon as I said the words, I wanted to take them back. I was wrong and she was right. I couldn't even imagine what it would be like if my dad left to live in Japan for a year—but I didn't think I could stand it! And I didn't want to go to the game with anyone but Lisa.

"I'm sorry. I didn't mean that," I apologized.

"It's all right," she answered in a voice that let me know it really wasn't. "I've got to hang up now." And before I could say anything else, she did.

On Monday morning at school, Lisa wouldn't look at me. Actually, she didn't talk to anyone. She just stayed at her desk and stared at her books until lunch. In the cafeteria, she sat at a table by herself. I gathered up my courage and sat next to her anyway.

"I really am sorry about what I said on the phone," I began. "I was a jerk. It's just that I wanted you to come so much. And I thought the break would do you good."

"It's okay," she answered. "I'm just so nervous about this contest. But it's almost over now. The essays are due at Molson's on Wednesday. They're going to print the winning essay in the newspaper next Saturday."

"I'll keep my fingers crossed for you."

"Thanks." Lisa finally smiled. "So, who went with you to the basketball game?"

Part of me had been dying to tell her. The other part was mortified. "Swear you won't tell anyone?"

"On my life." She crossed her heart.

"Jonathan came with us."

"Jonathan!" she squealed. *"You gave the extra ticket to Jonathan?"*

I put my hand over her mouth. "He was the only one I could think of who likes basketball."

"Matt and Paul like basketball. How come you didn't ask one of them?" she teased.

"Jonathan's all right when you get to know him." I left out the part about his eyes.

"Yeah, sure." Lisa was obviously unconvinced. She looked down at her uneaten lunch. "I guess I'm not very hungry. Do you want to go outside?"

"Okay." But first I took a Colonel Crunch bar out of my pocket and unwrapped it. I broke it in two and offered her half. She took a bite, and then we went out to the school yard.

In class that afternoon, Mr. Popper asked me if I could stay a few minutes after school.

"This isn't exactly about you, Amanda," he explained, after everyone had left. "It's more about being a friend. I think something is wrong with Lisa. She's so quiet and sad lately. I've asked her if I can help, but she says it's nothing. Well, it doesn't seem like nothing to me, but I don't want to worry her mother unnecessarily."

I swallowed hard. "What can I do about it?"

Mr. Popper smiled. "Just continue being a good friend and encourage her to talk about her problems. If whatever is troubling Lisa is really serious, try to get her to talk to an adult."

I wanted to blurt out everything to Mr. P. Maybe he could even help Lisa finish her essay. But I knew she would be furious if I told him her secret. She would probably never speak to me again. So I decided to wait until the next Saturday before I did anything. If she won the contest, she'd go back to acting normal. If she didn't . . . well, then I'd see.

"Lisa's okay," I told him. It was hard for me to meet his eyes. "She'll be fine after next Saturday. She's expecting a big surprise."

"A surprise is something you don't expect," Mr. Popper said, gently.

"Right. I meant, she'll be surprised if she gets . . . it."

Mr. Popper looked as if he might laugh. I figured it was a good time to leave. "Can I please go now?" I asked, looking at the clock.

"Of course."

When I got outside, Jonathan was sitting on the steps.

"What are you still doing here?" I exclaimed.

"I thought maybe you were in trouble, since Mr. P. asked you to stay after school."

Jonathan actually cared that I might be in trouble! A kind of sweet warmth, like drinking hot chocolate, spread through my chest. But I couldn't possibly tell him what my talk with Mr. P. had been about. "Everything's okay," I said.

For a moment, he looked as if he didn't know what else to say. He kicked a pebble.

"How come Lisa didn't wait for you? You two don't seem to be together much anymore. Aren't you still friends?"

Suddenly it seemed like the whole world was interested in Lisa and me. "How come you're so busy minding my business?" I snapped.

He ignored me. "So what were you talking to Mr. Popper about just now?"

"Why is everyone so nosey all of a sudden!"

"Take it easy, Mandy. I was just wondering if maybe it had anything to do with me?"

"You! What are you talking about?"

"Nothing. Never mind." His ears got red.

Now it was my turn to be curious. Lately it seemed like everyone had a secret.

And
the Winner Is . . .

On Wednesday, the day Lisa's essay was due, she didn't come to school. I wondered if she was ill or just needed the time to rewrite the final copy. Unless she was very sick, her mother would be at work, so Lisa would still be able to keep the essay a secret.

I called as soon as I got home. "Hi, it's me. Are you really sick?"

"Well, my stomach is a little upset."

"Oh. I thought maybe you had to go to Molson's or something."

"Oh. Well, I did," she said quickly.

"Weren't you afraid your mother would call while you were out?"

"I took the phone off the hook. I figured I could tell her I'd been napping."

"Well, at least now you're finally free. Want to come over tomorrow?"

"I guess so."

She didn't sound very enthusiastic. I thought maybe her essay hadn't turned out as well as she'd hoped.

"I guess you're still nervous about whether you'll win," I said, as gently as I could.

"Let's just drop it," she answered. "Let's challenge the boys to a basketball game tomorrow."

That was more like the old Lisa I knew. "I think first we'd better spend some time practicing."

There were only ten days left until the following Saturday when the winning essay would be printed in the newspaper. Lisa and I spent most of them together, shooting hoops, baking pizza, and just hanging out. It was like we were making up for all the time we missed when she was writing her essay. But I didn't mention the contest again and neither did she.

When Saturday finally came, I awakened while it was still dark. I was determined to get to our newspaper before Mom or Dad. I waited, staring out the window, until the weak morning light began to show. Soon I saw the paperboy pedaling up the road, tossing papers onto lawns without even slowing down. The minute ours sailed through the air, I crept downstairs.

I brought the paper up to my room and locked the door. I wondered if Lisa was doing the same thing in her room. My fingers felt clumsy as I undid the rubber band around the rolled up paper. It was cold and a bit damp from its brief stay on the dewy lawn. There was a boxed message about the contest right on the front page: "Molson's Travel's Winning Essay!—page 28."

"Please let it be Lisa," I prayed as I turned the pages. When I got to page 28 and read the title, I almost fainted: "How Not to Act When Visiting a Farm—by Amanda Simon."

There in the paper was the report I'd written for my independent study project, cartoons and all! How did they ever get my essay? Someone must have sent it to Molson's Travel. But who? Why would anyone have done something like that?

What would Lisa think when she saw my name in the paper where hers should have been? Of course she would think I'd entered the essay myself! I would rather have died than entered it against Lisa's, but she'd never

believe that now. How could she help but hate me? Our friendship was over. Tears streamed down my face. How could this have happened?

I thought about waking Mom and Dad, but what could they do? It was hopeless, really hopeless. I got back into bed and pulled the covers over my head. I wanted this to be a dream. But the phone rang too loudly in the hall for it to be a dream. I looked at my clock. It was only 8:00 A.M. It was probably Lisa calling to say she despised me. I ran to get it.

"Lisa?" I whispered into the receiver. I felt dizzy with nervousness.

"Wrong. Guess again," a voice answered. "There's a surprise for you in this morning's paper."

"Who is this?" The voice sounded familiar, but I was confused.

"It's Jonathan."

"Jonathan? You mean you saw my essay in the paper already?"

"You saw it too? I didn't even know you read the paper." He was silent for a second. "You know, for someone who just won a contest, you don't sound very happy. I thought you'd love winning a trip to Japan. You've always

seemed so interested in that country. I remembered that you brought all those brochures to
school."

A picture of myself and Jonathan in the
coatroom flashed through my mind. I was
pushing my Japan pamphlets into his hands
to hide the cap bombs from the sub. All of a
sudden, I had an idea what had happened.
"You sent my essay to Molson's!" I squealed.

"Uh-huh!" he said, sounding pleased. "When
I saw the ad about the contest, I thought of
your farm report right away. It was really
funny, even the part about me. I figured entering it for you would be a great way of thank-
ing you for saving R.J.'s life. If you won, that
is. Which you did." He paused for breath.

I was too shocked to say anything.

"After I saw the ad, I asked Mr. P. if he'd
give me your report to send. He said first I'd
have to ask your mother and father if it was
okay with them."

"You mean they knew?" I gasped. This was
incredible!

"Sure! Your mom thought it was a fantastic
idea. She even said if you won, maybe she and
your dad would buy two extra tickets so your
whole family could go. She told me she's writ-

ing an article about family vacations, anyway. Aren't you even going to thank me?"

"You don't understand," I wailed. "Because of this, I've probably lost my best friend forever!"

"You mean Lisa? What are you talking about?"

"Lisa entered the contest, too," I explained. "She wanted to win a trip to Japan so she could visit her father. He's working there, and she's been worried that she won't ever get to see him. It was supposed to be a secret. She didn't even want her mother to know." I began sniffling again. "Now she probably hates me."

"Gee, I'm sorry, Mandy." Jonathan sounded shocked. "I didn't know Lisa was entering, too."

"Nobody knew except me."

"What are you going to do now?"

"I don't know. I guess if Lisa will let me, I'll just give her the tickets. But she might not take them. I've got to go. I need to think about this some more."

I hung up and turned around. Mom was sitting on the steps in her bathrobe. She smiled sympathetically and patted a place next to her. I went over and sat down.

"Oh Mom, what am I going to do?" I cried.

"Don't worry, we'll figure something out." She smoothed my hair. "Poor Mandy! You only meant to be a good friend."

For a long time, we sat together on the steps. It felt good to know I wasn't alone anymore. "We might as well get dressed and have some breakfast," Mom finally said. "We'll be able to think better on a full stomach."

I went back to my room and put on some clothes. I was just finishing dressing when the doorbell rang.

"Now who could that be at this hour?" I heard Mom say, as she ran to get it. I went into the hall to listen. Dad and Tammy came out of their rooms, too.

"What's going on?" Tammy wanted to know.

Before I could answer, Mom called up the stairs. "Mandy, you have visitors!"

Until then, I thought I couldn't possibly feel any worse, but now I did. Who else could it be but Lisa, here to end our friendship in person. I wiped my eyes on my sleeve and trudged down the stairs.

Sure enough, Lisa was there in the kitchen. And so were Mrs. Krauss, Mr. Popper, and Jonathan. When I saw them I started crying all over again.

"It's okay, Amanda," Mr. Popper said. "It's been a terrible mix-up, that's all. After Jonathan spoke to you this morning, he called me. Then I went to talk to Lisa and Mrs. Krauss. We decided to come here so we could all work it out together."

"Oh, Lisa, I'm so sorry," I wailed. "You can have my tickets to Japan. I don't want them! I didn't enter my essay, Jonathan did. And I didn't mean to tell anyone about you entering, either. I just couldn't help it when Jonathan called."

"I know," Lisa said, quietly. She took a deep breath. "I have something to tell you, too. I never did send an essay to Molson's."

"You didn't? But you've worked so hard on it! All you've done is write for the last three weeks!"

Now Lisa began crying, too. "I never really wrote anything but a few sentences. I tried and tried, but it never came out right. I couldn't do it, no matter how long I sat at my desk. I was too ashamed to tell you."

Lisa's mother put her arm around her. "Lisa was just so anxious about her dad's being away. . . ." She looked at Lisa. "I'm sorry, darling. I guess your father or I should have thought to explain to you sooner that his company is going to pay for your trip to visit him this summer. We just didn't realize you'd been worrying about it so."

"Well, it looks like you're *both* going to Japan," Jonathan said, grinning wildly. "Just don't forget to send R.J. a postcard."

"Are you two going to cry anymore?" Tammy asked.

Lisa and I looked at each other and smiled. Then we hugged.

"I think this calls for some chocolate chip pancakes," Mom announced.

"Let's go out and shoot baskets afterward," Jonathan suggested. "I'll challenge each of you."

"Great!" Lisa had been itching for a chance to play against him. They turned to me for an answer.

"Sure," I agreed. Who knew? The way my luck was going lately, maybe I'd win.

Dear R.J.,
Guess what? Cameras are a
bargain in Japan. Mom and Dad
bought me a 35-millimeter to
replace the old one that drowned
on Mr. P's farm. I'll take lots of
pictures to show you and Jonathan
when I get home. I'll try to find
a Japanese rooster. See you soon!
            Your friend,
            Mandy

Jonathan Adler
22 Birch St.
Hartman, N.Y.
      USA